Berthold Auerbach, Clara Bell

Brigitta

A Tale

Berthold Auerbach, Clara Bell

Brigitta
A Tale

ISBN/EAN: 9783337072063

Printed in Europe, USA, Canada, Australia, Japan

Cover: Foto ©Andreas Hilbeck / pixelio.de

More available books at **www.hansebooks.com**

BRIGITTA.

A TALE.

BY

BERTHOLD AUERBACH,

AUTHOR OF "ON THE HEIGHTS," ETC.

FROM THE GERMAN BY

CLARA BELL.

Copyright Edition.

LEIPZIG 1880

BERNHARD TAUCHNITZ.

LONDON: SAMPSON LOW, MARSTON, SEARLE & RIVINGTON.
CROWN BUILDINGS, 188, FLEET STREET.
PARIS: C. REINWALD, 15, RUE DES SAINTS PÈRES.

BRIGITTA.

THE GOLDEN LAMB

is the name written up on the sign that pro-
jects from the wall, and the fat gilt lamb hangs
its head bashfully, but with a slight and as it
were inquisitive twist on one side. I smell
the aroma—pungent and bitter, but refreshing
too—of pressed wild cherries whenever I remember the inn on the country high road.

It is the time of year when summer is fad-
ing into autumn; in the meadows the aftermath
is being mown in the valley through which the
mountain stream—navigable for timber rafts—
tumbles over the sluices; now and again I hear
the whetting of the scythe, and a passing gleam
of reflected sunshine flashes from the blade. In
the walnut trees behind the house and in the

sweet chesnuts higher up the slope, the nut-
hatches are whisking and flying to and fro; the
trout in the mountain brook, which is so clear
that you may see the bottom, swim merrily up
and down, never dreaming of their companions
imprisoned in the floating tank that is chained
to the shore. A fresh atmosphere of water, field,
and meadow breathes round the house—it is to
be wished that some such air might be wafted
across these pages and pervade my story.

Aye! there are still to be found in retired spots
such peaceful and thriving inns, kept up with
primitive and genial hospitality, and one of the
most comfortable is the Golden Lamb. The
spacious one-storied house stands back a little
way from the high-road to leave room for the
vehicles that stop at its door; formerly above a
dozen of moveable mangers stood here, so
that loaded horses might feed without being
unharnessed.

Those who came down from the mountains
could here congratulate themselves on having
reached the valley, and those who were going

up the mountain, and wanted additional horses would recruit themselves as well, by a good measure of liquor of indigenous growth, much relished _by the native taste. The fire blazed cheerily in the kitchen; and was there not a better savour then than now, when a tunnel has been cut through the mountain? As I write the train comes snorting in, gives one shrill screaming halloo, then it is swallowed up by the mountain, and again all is still. But even now there often comes a timber cart slowly creaking down, or a more rapid Bernese waggonette with well-to-do men and women in the costume of the country; if they are returning from a funeral they halt awhile, and have wine brought out to them; if they are going home from some jollification they nod to the host and drive on —they have had enough for to-day.——

The rafts-men, who bring down the trunks of timber from the upper part of the valley, are always' ready to lean their long steering poles against the house wall in token that here they tarry awhile; they appreciate the good food and

pure wholesome wine of the house, and are glad
to arrange so that they can pass a night here.
The weather-beaten and gigantic figures of the
rafts-men sit in the' large eating-room, with its
stove of glazed green tiles and its loudly ticking
Black-Forest clock; they clean and brush themselves up before they sit down to the long table
on which they prop themselves with their bare
and massive arms, and devour huge pieces of
fat meat and heaped spoonfuls of thick horse-
radish porridge; nor, of course, is the liquor
neglected; an open wine-flask stands between
every two men, and is emptied and filled again
and again. At first they speak hardly a word;
they eat and drink silently, almost solemnly;
presently they begin, shouting as if across the
roar of waters; it is not without reason that it
has become proverbial of a man, who talks
piercingly loud: He has a voice like a rafts-
man.

Then, when the men are going to bed so as
to be ready to start early before day-break, the
hostess says in her persuasive but decided tones:

"Softly there, you men, we have a wonderful learned writer here in the house—he is a light sleeper and needs rest." And the strong men pull off their high rafts-men's boots, and creep noiselessly up in their stockings to the room under the roof, and come down again just as softly next morning. Yes, for the hostess knows what a blessed refuge and remedy is quiet, and she knows too what a nervous man requires; she has learned it by much experience.

But it shall not be told where the hostelry of the Golden Lamb is to be found, or it will be distinguished with a star in the guide books, and within a twelvemonth Englishmen in plaids and Englishwomen in red shawls will have scared away its homelike repose; and instead of the simple but perfectly neat Agnes some black-coated Jean, at odds with his destiny, will wait upon us; and the genuine honey—every thing is called genuine in these days—the honey made by the bees in the kitchen garden, will run short and sham honey will be set before us. And, worst disaster of all, a piano will be·

brought into the house, and the guests who are
waiting for their dinner or who have satisfied
their appetites, will strum upon it to kill their
own time and the peace of the hearers. No—
the world need not know of that inn; the hosts
are pleased when guests arrive but they are not
disheartened when they stop away, for they are
not mere inn-keepers; they have fields and pasture and wood, and those who are lucky enough
to stay at the Lamb have it said to them: "You
are in good quarters; neither man nor wife has
an enemy far or near; they never had but one,
and the wife did more good to him than could
be thought possible."

The people round about talk much more of
the wife than of the husband; she treats all the
peasant folk as if she were perfectly and merely
their equal, and that without any constraint or
effort, for at heart she is still a simple peasant
child, though she has made acquaintance with a
large part of the world even in the highest
circles, and owns many books of the best class,
which she has read and understood. The hus-

band is well pleased that his wife should be
more thought of than himself, but he deserves
the highest respect, and he has it too.   Still he
needs no praise from strangers; he is content
with the esteem of one human soul, and it may
well suffice him.

There, she has come out of the house, and
is standing with a peasant in the costume of the
Oberland on the door-step.   She is tall and
slight, and has one of those faces in which we
see how many sorrows have marked them; but
now respite and peace dwell there, and the
brown eyes, which still have the clear sparkle
of youth, have a look of security and of steady
kindliness.   She holds herself stiffly erect, nay
she even holds her head somewhat loftily; her
demeanour betrays the daughter of a soldier,
and perhaps something of the independence of
a peasant of rank.   She holds out her hand to
the man, and says: "Good-bye, come again;
and give our remembrances to all at home who
still remember us."

She goes in doors again, for the host of the

Lamb is coming up from the conduit—a middle aged man, somewhat stout but still active nevertheless. He is walking cautiously and with little steps, for he has a tub of water on his shoulders which he carries into the distillery on the ground-floor where he is making Kirschwasser; he only casts a passing glance at the pigs which are grunting and routing among the skins and stones that have been cast out, and shoving each other in play, as if they would fain shout for joy.

When mine host of the Lamb gets confidential with a guest—and he is not free from suspiciousness—he fetches out the red morocco cases in which lie five prize medals awarded to him at different great exhibitions; the one from Paris he shows last. Which of them he values most he does not let out, for he is an inn-keeper, and he has learned in Switzerland to keep on good terms with all nationalities. At the same time he is fully convinced that pure Kirschwasser is a perfect panacea—not only does it warm, says he; but it cools you afterwards. When the

goodness of his liquor is praised, he never fails
to say: "I learned how to make it from my
father; there is a particular knack in it."

He is honestly proud of his fame as a dis-
tiller of Kirschwasser, but otherwise does not
set much value on the opinion of the world, for,
as has been said, there is one human soul that
esteems him highly, and with that he is content
and may well remain content.

Now let us hear the wife herself.

CHAPTER I.

WELL, my husband says I am to tell you everything; and so it shall be. I will dig it all out to the very last root; confess both the good and the evil, and the one is as true as the other.

People say of me that I have fulfilled the hardest of all the commandments: Love your enemies—I am not so good though, as people think; one man passes for better than he is, and another for worse.

My husband is not much to look at, but any one who really knows him and all our history must say: All honour to such a man. There may be others more clever and finer fellows, but there is not an honester nor a better; and sensible too at bottom, except on one point; he still looks back with proud delight on the day when I, the daughter of a head-peasant, took him for my husband, and when he wants to do himself special honour he calls me the princess of Schlehenhof.

I was born at Schlehenhof, but the house is no longer to be seen by mortal eye; where it once stood forest trees now grow.

High up on the road to the lake of Constance, on the ridge just before it slopes down into the valley, you may see that in the midst of the dark pine-forest there is one light green tree; that is the hollow lime tree by the ruined well, the only trace left that once men dwelt on the spot. I went back there once, about two years ago, but ten horses would not drag me there again. Memory, to be sure, is stronger than ten horses, and it often carries me back there of its own accord, both in my dreams and awake; and I see the house again, roomy and large, with its thick straw thatch and the brown beams of which it was built; at the side facing the morning sun there are a number of windows close together; you may come down the hill side straight into the upper lofts. Close by are the stables where the horses rattle their chains, and I hear the great bell of the cow that leads the herd, and the tinkling bell of the black buck-goat, and the starlings twittering in the lime-tree by the well.

It was said that our house was the oldest in all the country-side, it certainly was one of the coldest; but we never found it out, the living room was heated the whole year round, and we had plenty of wood; several hundred acres of forest—I don't know how many—belonged to our farm. It was my mother's property; my father was the elder son of the head-peasant; the younger, my uncle Donatus, had his father's estate, and my father wished to add to the pro-perty he had married into, and that is just how it all fell out * * *

There was an orchard to the house and a few fields round it, but not much land. We only grew oats and potatoes up there, hay we sold, and food-grains we had to buy, for the few fields we had down in the village did not suffice for our household-use with all the servants and day-labourers. When at any time a family died out or quitted the village, my father did not buy the fields that were to be sold ; he said that poorer folks ought sometimes to have a chance of settling on the land. He meant well to his fellow men even if he did not express himself so in words. He was quite content till—but I will tell you about that when I come to it.

At that time—the whole history takes me back thirty years—at that time there was a road from the village up to our house, now there is only a foot-path ; the government has had a path cut through the wood about half way up, and the forest stretches away and closes you in ; for miles round, they say, a squirrel can leap now from tree to tree.

It was lonely up at Schlehenhof, but when you are used to it you don't want neighbours. Often a butcher, a wood merchant or a cattle dealer would come there, and in the autumn the cabbage cutter with his tools, and the harness-maker too we used to take into the

house; our house-dog would never cease barking
so long as a strange man was outside. In the
evenings my father used to smoke and my
mother to spin; we always grew hemp in one
field near the village and it was spun in the
house; my mother was always particularly
pleased when the weaver came to fetch the yarn;
sewing yarn she always twisted herself, on a
ring that was fastened to a beam in the ceil-
ing.

When I went to school I read a great deal
aloud out of my school-books; I was always
fond of reading. My mother, by the recom-
mendation of the parson, had subscribed to a
History of the Saints, and every month a yellow-
covered number came in, full of pictures. I read
aloud out of that too, but not very willingly; I
seemed to feel in my own person all the torments
and sufferings these innocent and godly men
must have suffered, and often screamed out in
my sleep, for all that was so horribly shewn
there came home to me with such reality that
I was quite terrified and miserable. Then my

father forbid that such things should be read in the evening for the future, and what my father said was said once for all. Not that he talked much in general, and he let my mother rule, particularly over us children.

My father's name was Alexander—Xander they say in our part; he had served in a regiment of chasseurs, with the great bear-skin caps; this regiment has long ceased to exist, but father was very proud of his honourable discharge which hung against the wall in a gilt frame. Aye, my father set great store by that, and it came to be a misfortune to him and to us.

There were five of us, brothers and sisters; three died young, and mother often said—but only to strangers and when my father was not by—that the farm was too bleak; in old times perhaps men might have endured it better; but now folks are not so strong. She too used to cough a great deal. I am the youngest, and I grew up in easy circumstances and in perfect contentment till my thirteenth year. There was peace in our house, not mirth—we worked, prayed, eat, and slept. We had six—nay often eight—horses in the stable and reared the foals ourselves. Schmaje, a dealer, brought my father the beasts he wanted, and took away those he did not want and that were no longer of use to us. Father worked with the men like one of themselves, and we carried the trunks down to the saw-mill, and carted the fire-wood to market with our own horses.

My father had also planted an oak copse—I think it was Jorns, the forester, who was then a young man, who advised him—up on the high plain where there had been fields before, but they had not yielded much produce. The oak bark brought a good deal of money, and the only gay time we had was in the spring when the girls who barked the oak used to sing. Bonifacia, the road-mender's wife, was always there, and she knew most songs, and I and my elder sister used to help too, and I have a number of songs in my memory from that time; they often haunt my memory, and then a feeling comes over me as if I smelt the sap of the young oaks.

On Sundays we used to drive to church—it was nearly an hour's ride—my sister and I on the back seat and father and mother on the front seat; our white horses were harnessed with beautiful trappings and we rode in quite proudly. Hardly a word would be spoken, people even forget to speak, in the midst of loneliness.

My father had no intimate companions, he rarely went into the public room at the Angel where our horses were put up; if his pipe was full he was content, and if a comrade from his regiment spoke to him he offered him his tobacco-pouch that he might fill his own; cigars were not known in our parts at that time. My father was chairman of the parish committee, they would gladly have made him a member of the town council, but we lived too far off; a man is of no use in that way unless he lives near the church, the town-hall and the school-house, where people can easily come

about their affairs. While my father was at the
town-hall, mother would go with us two girls
to see poor people; she liked to have us with
her when she was doing good, and the poor
folks often said to us: "Aye, children—things are
sure to go well with you; your mother's good
deeds are sure to be rewarded in you." Then
mother would look at us, and her eyes would
fill with tears, she was a very tender-hearted
soul.

Who could have foreseen how things would
fall out and that I should be the only one left,
and after so much trouble should come to such
a good end as I have at last?

CHAPTER II.

THE last house in the village next to our farm was that of the road-mender, whose business it is in our parts to keep the roads in order. Everything about the house was neat and clean; in his little garden were the earliest and latest flowers and trimly kept beds of vegetables, and in the little rooms everything was as tidy as a doll's house; Bonifacia had always time for everything and was always decently clad. Certainly she had no one in the house but her husband; her only son Ronymus was in service with us; Bonifacia had formerly been a maid with us, and she clung to us as if she were still one of our servants; in joy and in trouble Bonifacia was sent for and was there in an instant. Mother never went past the road-keeper's little house without turning in; she had a very high opinion of the man, who was not thought much of but was thoroughly sensible and upright. Bonifacia never would allow herself to accept any present; "Mistress," she used to say, "all the presents you would wish to give me may stay with you; I will go to fetch them some day when I am in want of them." But she never came to us—quite the reverse.

When my sister was married Bonifacia was in the house with us again and helped to arrange everything; she could be trusted with all the keys and knew where everything was. My sister married young—much too young—the son of the inn-keeper of the Angel in the village. My father gave her a large dowry all in hard bright coin; I held open the sack with both hands while the gold and silver were poured in. I had heard it said that it would bring luck if the hand of an innocent child touched it.

I had a new dress for my sister's wedding, a costume such as we wore in our part of the country; you hardly see it worn at all now. Never in my life was I prouder than that day,

when the music went first and we followed, and
the lads fired their guns till the mountains re-
echoed again and again. My uncle Donatus
and all our great clan of relatives were there
together, and I felt as if every one was looking
at nothing else but me and my beautiful
clothes. My sister cried and it was looked
upon as a good omen, but it did not turn
out so.

They were all merry enough at the wedding-
supper. The trumpeter of the band had been
in the regiment of chasseurs, and my father got
him to play the réveil and whistled to the
tune—I never saw him so full of spirits; I feel
as if it had been his last really gay and jovial
hour, for all those that came after were not
really and truly gay. I remember quite positively that father spoke then of his captain in
the regiment, Baron Haueisen; what he said of
him I quite forget, but the name dwelt in my
memory from that time.

I went away from the wedding-feast and
stood out by the house-door, and a woman and

a man—I did not know them—were talking together. The man said: "She is now Xander's
only child, she will have the whole of the big
farm some day, she is the princess of Schlehenhof and may pick the best peasant-prince for
her husband."   `

I, a peasant-princess! and I may win a
peasant-prince! it struck my fancy like a light-
ning-flash. Aye—out there in the door-way,
an overweening pride came upon me, and seeing
several beggars and cripples, who had gathered
together from the whole country round to the
house where a wedding was going forward, I
went to my brother-in-law and begged him to
give me some money; he gave me some, and I
distributed among the poor people. My first
childish act of benevolence was sheer pride.

Now too I went to school; the way to our
village was long, and until I was fifteen I was
weakly and small; it was only in misery that I
shot up so tall. I staid with my sister the first
year of my schooling, but I was dreadfully home-
sick for our own homestead. In the inn, where

so many people were going in and out, where every one might sit were he liked, and halloo and bawl and give orders, I was not happy; if only I had seen a horse from our farm I would gladly have mounted him and have said to him: This evening you shall go home again.

My sister died at the birth of her first child; Agnes, who is with us now, is my sister's only child. She is a widow and has had a hard life too, that is why she is so shy and scared. She was only married a quarter of a year, but that was long enough for her husband to squander all her dowry, then he went mad; for years he was in a mad house and then he died. Aye, the world is full of misery. If you pick out a single family and all the ins and outs of its belongings, you find all is sorrow——

When my sister was dead I went home again—but, such is man! never content. Now our farm was too lonely for me, and the way to school was so long. But things very soon came right again.

At first to be sure I could hardly take in

the idea that my sister lay under the hillock in the churchyard, that she never came near us, nor troubled herself about her child and her only sister; but when we are young we soon forget again—and that is well. I was gay and I sang on my way to and fro like any other child of twelve or thirteen. My mother wished to take her little grandchild Agnes into her own care, but my brother-in-law took it with him when he married again, into Switzerland. Who could have thought then that the time would come when I should live in Switzerland for many years?

CHAPTER III.

ONE day Jorns, the forester, rode up to our house on his dappled grey horse. He was but young then, but already highly respected; the worthy man had to take serious matters upon himself, and afterwards with his son-in-law he had to shoot the son of Bergschinder. I shall have more to tell about Bergschinder.

Old Jorns lives now with his son, and his daughter Carla and her husband in the hunting lodge that has been turned into a school for foresters. It is often said in the inn-parlour what a fine man he was and universally loved. I shall never forget him as I saw him then, wherever he went joy and honour went with him, and so they seemed to enter our room as he came in. He sat down at the table and said: "Schlchhof,* call your wife, Master; I have something to say to you both."

* Calling him by the name of his homestead.

My mother could scarcely cease speaking of
the honour and pleasure of such a visit, but the
forester said with a smile: "That is all very
well, but what will you say to my having come
to turn you out of house and home? Aye—I
believe the plainest way is the best with you.
Well then, the short of it is, I have a commission from the government to purchase your
farm of you. I need no go-between with you;
I am a plain honest man, and with you I can
deal honestly. We will make a valuation of
the farm according to justice and equity, and
pay cash down."

My father and mother looked at each other,
and my father said:

"Well, mistress, what do you think of it?"

My mother was coughing badly, and the
forester said:

"Her cough is answer enough. The farm is
too bleak; for five months, from the beginning
of winter till Candlemas, the sun never shines
on your roof; men cannot thrive here, it is a
place only fit for wild beasts."

"What do you mean by that?" asked my father.

"Simply that we want to throw your farmstead into the forest again."

"What! and how could we answer for such a deed to those who dwelt here before us?"

"Well, well," said my mother. "And if the arrangement is a good one, why not?"

"And you say so?" cried father. "And it was your forbears who sat here—not mine? For my part what I say is this: With all respect to your honour and to your honour's proposal, he that sits firm has no call to move, and I don't stir. If my wife chooses—"

"I—I have thought many a time that Heaven bends over all the world—"

She would have liked to say more, but she broke off and the forester did not help her out; he insisted that nothing binding should be settled at present, that my parents should consider of the matter between themselves and let him know their answer. So matters stood, and when the forester had ridden off, father came back into the parlour and told mother that she ought to have been more determined against it, for then they would have got a better price; when he saw me he sent me out of the room. I stood outside in front of the house and looked at the house and the fields and the forest, and could not help wondering how any one could sell the place and go away, I could not understand it.

When I went into the sitting-room at supper-time, I asked when our farm was to be sold and where we should go to, but mother said, and she looked at my father: "We shall not sell it; we shall stay here where our fathers lived before us and grew to old age, hale and hearty."

CHAPTER IV.

IT was a lovely autumn day; down in the valley the trees were already sprinkled with yellow leaves—up at our place the cherries were only just ripe. I was going home from school; I had slung my satchel on my arm and was singing as I went. I cannot remember the whole of the song now, but the end ran thus:

> "The cherries they be black and red,
> And I love my love till I be dead."

That is how a child sings and does not know what it is singing.

On the way we had a field, and Ronymus was just ploughing it with our white horses; the plough slipped on easily, Ronymus whistled as he went, and when he saw me as he turned, he called out to me that if I would wait an hour I could ride home on the waggon; for the plough could not be dragged so far, it had to be loaded on a cart. I did not care to ride, so I went on and was as merry as any child can be. Presently I heard something behind me; I turned round, and there was a magnificent one horse chaise coming, so light and smart that you could not tell what it was made of and how it could hold together. It was a two-wheeled carriage, almost like a light cart, but high and slight; a bay horse with a black mane and black tail—the hair streamed in the wind—was harnessed in front, and in it sat a man with a military cap, or to speak exactly, he stood. I stood still, the carriage came nearer; the man had a long moustache stiffened out on each side like a cat's whiskers, and his eyes were green—no, it was only that he had green spectacles. The reins with which he guided the horse were of snowy whiteness, and he had on white gloves.

I stood transfixed, as if I could not stir from the spot. Where was he going? the road led only to our house. The horse, the

man and the chaise came nearer and nearer;
the man asked me:

"Child—where are you going?"

I was frightened out of my wits—we had
grown very shy of men up at our lonely
homestead. He asked me again, and I said:

"Up to Schlchenhof."

"Do you live there?"

"Aye, I do."

"Who do you belong to?"

"The master there."

"What is his name?"

"Xander."

With one spring the man was out of the
chaise—he had on high, shining boots.

"Come, child," said he. "I will drive you
up to your father's at the farm."

I could not utter a word; he put his arm
round me and tossed me up like a ball into
the fine carriage, sprang up himself and whish!
off we flew again. I felt as if I had been
carried away into fairy land by the prince who

3*

fetches the goose-girl and bears her off to his castle of pure gold, diamonds, and pearls.

The man asked me how old I was, and I told him I was going on for thirteen. "You are but a little one," said he, and he took my hand and said: "Judging by your fingers you ought to grow tall; you may be as tall as your father!" This prophecy — which came true — delighted me much, for I did not at all wish to remain so small.

I asked him why he wore green spectacles, and when he explained to me that he had bad eyes, I told him how I had had bad eyes too, but Cordula, the carrier — whom they used to call the Weekly News — had cured me by making me hold a new laid egg while it was still warm on my eyes. "I will do that; thank you," said the man.

By this time I had lost all my fear, and was truly delighted to think that I could cure anybody, and such a fine gentleman too; and I went on to say that I washed my eyes with water in which oak-bark had been boiled. Aye! my eye-doctoring began early in my life.

I was now quite intimate with the man, and asked him why he had the cut in his cheek reaching almost from his ear to the corner of his mouth; he laughed — but that cheek did not laugh too — and said that a pistol-shot had once gone along through it. I looked again at the man who had once been so nearly shot.

As we went up the hill towards our farmstead, I must need show him my school copybook; he praised me for being able to write so beautifully, and I told him I could reckon in my head better still. He gave me some sums to do, and I worked them all out, and then he said:

"You are quite a clever girl, and a pretty one too."

Ah! I was still no more than a child, but there is nothing worse for a child than to have such things said to it. The serpent in Paradise, no doubt, said to Eve: Oh! how fair, how beautiful you are! To be sure, he could not then have said: You are handsomer than such or such a one—and that is what really makes the flattery sweetest.

———

CHAPTER V.

WE stopped at the farm; my father saw us out of the window, and called out:

"Hey! who comes here?"

"Have you forgotten me—don't you know me?" replied the man.

"What, you, Sir—the Captain!" cried my father; and he came down, bringing a chair for him to get out on, and holding his hat in his hand; but the Captain laughed:

"Old comrade, I don't want the chair, I can still leap and vault; but before I get out I must ask a favour of you—give me your child there. We have no children, and I should like just such another."

"Your honour is pleased to be joking," said father laughing. He lifted me down and stroked my cheeks, a thing he had never done before. I stood on the ground feeling as if I had fallen from heaven. This then is father's Captain—and I am a pretty girl! I went indoors into our bed-room, mounted on a bench and looked at myself in the glass; I stroked my own cheeks—aye, I am pretty—and clever —and 'a peasant princess into the bargain.

I heard my father and the Captain talking in the parlour. I hastily undressed myself, washed and rubbed myself, and put on my beautiful dress that I had had for my sister's wedding. My mother came in and asked: "And what are you about?"

"Aye, mother, I must dress myself a little better before his honour the grand gentleman."

"As to whether he is a grand gentleman or not I cannot say, but at any rate we need not try to seem anything before him but what we are."

I went down with my mother into the sitting-room; the Captain was saying: "Xander, either you must be familiar and friendly with me, or I must be on ceremony with you."* My father looked straight before him, and the man went on:

"Well, then we must stand on ceremony, but be none the less good friends. But at any rate pray do not call me Captain, I will not be called so any longer. You know my name of course."

"Oh, certainly," answered father. "You see it is always under my eyes and those of my family." He pointed to the wall on which hung his discharge, where the Captain's name was to be seen. Oh! if only we had known at that time why the man was so friendly and affable. But what had to be, had to be——

Mother too asked why he wore green spectacles, and he said he had bad eyes, but he did not like to speak of them, for as soon as he mentioned them they hurt him. Mother found it just the same with her own aches and pains,

---

* Expressed in German by the familiar *Du* or the ceremonious *Sie*.

and the Captain could tell her just how she
suffered and yet never showed it. Mother
looked at father, as much as to say, 'Here is a
knowing fellow, why he understands my complaints better than all the doctors.' Mother
looked at the Captain as if he had the gift of
divination. The Captain had now taken off his
spectacles, and his eyes were as beautiful as
a blue gem on which the sun shines; I cannot tell you how beautiful they were. He
went into the stable with my father, and mother
said to me:

"Come, we will put on our Sunday clothes
in honour of the gentleman."

Father sent in word from the stable that he
was going into the forest with the Captain, and
then we set to work to roast and boil; the
parlour was clean-swept and a shining clean
table-cloth was laid; a hunting scene was woven
in it and it had come down to us from my
grandmother's store; mother took the discharge
down from the wall and rubbed it up. Then the
men came in, and at dinner the Captain said:

"My dear friend, you are one of the most fortunate men in the world. You have a house full of plenty, a good wife and a blooming child. I wish I were a peasant like you."

Father stroked down the smooth table-cloth and nodded to himself, and mother said:

"We ought to be thankful to be reminded now and then how well off we are—it is so easy to forget it. Of course there are ups and downs in every life; it is all hill and dale in this world, my father used to say—he was master-beadle for two and thirty years—mayor you would call it now-a-days."

"Begging your honour's pardon, Captain," said my father. "Did you come merely to pay me a visit?"

"You are right to put a plain question, and I will give you a plain answer: No, not for that only. I heard that you wished to sell your farm to the government, or at any rate the forest. I am a man of business myself now, I must have something to do; I always give two

hundred gulden more than Government offers.
But I say to you now: "make no change, stay
on your own lot and plot, here you are the
real master." And then he told us that he
had been doing business with the peasant-pro-
prietor of Himbeerhof, that he was a great
speculator, but where money might be won
money might also be lost. They had now en-
tered into partnership to deliver a large quantity
of railway sleepers.

"I could make sleepers too," said father, and
the Captain agreed:

"Certainly you could, perfectly. Your trees
have mossy beards — they must be shaved.
Mistress, your forbears must have been rich
and righteous folks to have left you such a
forest to inherit; you have no idea what an
amount of dead capital is lying buried in your
woods."

It was late and I had to go to bed, but I
lay long awake and thinking: What on earth is
dead capital? Is it perhaps a buried treasure
which must be dug up secretly and without

uttering a word, at midnight, when the moon is full? At last I heard the Captain rise, I heard some talk about a black horse, and then my mother said his honour the Baron must come again and bring his wife with him and give us a chance of earning something as well as the master of Himbeerhof. What he answered I could not hear, only these words:

"Then I have your promise, you will not sell anything without giving me the first refusal of it. Now—good-bye—and give my love to your little daughter. What is her name?"

"Brigitta," shouted I from the bed-room, and the man laughed and my mother scolded me. Soon the chaise rolled past the house, and all was silent.

CHAPTER VI.

NEXT day, I was standing under the pent-house with Ronymus, who was polishing up the harness, and he told me that the Captain had given him a gold piece 'to drink his health with' at the sale of the horse, and that if only the Captain had been still in the army he would have volunteered to serve in his regiment. While we were standing there together Schmaje came up; he was the Jew, whom my father trusted entirely; he understood everything, and father was always glad to give him a turn; he always knew what father needed and brought him the best of everything. He asked Ronymus what the Captain had paid for the black horse.

"And if I were to tell you more than he did, would you believe me?"

"You cannot tell me more than is true,"

said Schmaje. "For you are not a liar by nature."

But he could not get anything out of Ronymus; he had not been told to tell, and 'he who holds his tongue cannot be forsworn.'

"He is a shrewd chap and an honest servant," said Schmaje, turning to me. Then father came up and asked Schmaje whether he he would cash the draft the Captain had left; Schmaje was ready to pay money down, he had cash with him, and when he saw the cheque he said he would buy the other black horse, he wanted one and he would give a Carolin* more. Father agreed; they went together into the sitting-room and I went with them; Schmaje then went on to say that he had heard that my father meant to sell the farm to the Government; Jews were forbidden by law to deal in real property even as middlemen, but perhaps he might be of use 'under the rose.' Of course there was nothing to be done with Jorns, but perhaps it

* About a pound sterling.

might be possible to learn beforehand who was to appraise it, and Government had certainly money enough. He looked keenly at my father as he spoke, but father said nothing and gave no sign ; then mother came in and Schmaje went on to say that he knew of a property in Breisgau where, as the saying is, you had all the five Ws—'Weald, Water, Wood, Wheat and Wine,' and besides that a good homestead, a large house where not a nail wanted driving, and all to be had for half its value.

"I am not going to sell," said my father. "I don't know what all this talk is about ; it is as if the birds as they fly across country had been chattering to every one, and none of it true."

"What isn't true, may become true," said Schmaje, and he looked at mother. She said that at any rate we might take the first opportunity of looking at the property in Breisgau, and Schmaje begged that she would only not mention his name in the matter; as there was a heavy penalty on any Jew, who took part in

such a transaction, but he considered it as safe
as if he had a bargain signed and sealed that
such honourable folks as the masters of
Schlehenhof would not leave him unremune-
rated. Then mother went on to ask how
matters generally stood with the captain;
Schmaje told her that he lived in a house that
was quite a little mansion, with a railing all
round it with spear-heads that were gilt; that
inside you walked on double carpets, that every
window was one single pane of glass, that the
vaulted stable was a perfect marvel, and the
horses eat out of mangers of white marble.
The captain had thrown up his commission —
people said all sorts of things about it — but it
was to carry on the business of his father-in-
law, who was dead and who had been a rich
banker in the capital. Some said he had come
into thousands of pounds, others declared that
he had inherited nothing but a rotten concern
which he was now trying to patch up with
the help of a certain retired lawyer, named
Schaller.

"What! is he mixed up with Bergschinder?" exclaimed my father. "I don't like that at all."

"Nor I neither," answered Schmaje. "Schaller is the bitterest enemy to the Jews—a perfect Haman; but the Captain is man enough to be a match for him, he is as crafty as he is well-bred."

As Schmaje rode off on the black horse, father said:

"I do not budge. All of a sudden it seems as if the whole world had come to seek me."

And so it was.

On Saturday came Cordula, the 'weekly news.' She had a donkey-cart, and the donkey must have particularly enjoyed its visits to our farm, for it always used to bray till the forest echoed again. Cordula dealt in butter and eggs, and she always had a great deal to talk over with my mother; she drove into the town once a week and brought us out sugar and coffee and salt—we wanted nothing else from the outside world. Then she told us too what was going on in the world, and to-day she informed us, how, on the way, she had turned into the Star-inn, and there was the Captain with his wife, who was very pretty and who had ridden off on a white horse and had a long blue dress on and a feather in her hat. They had been talking of Schlehenhof in the inn-parlour, and every one had agreed in praising the master and his wife and his child and everything about the place, so that the Baroness had said: "I must go there too some day."

Something else new happened that Saturday; the barber came, and father, who had always been close-shaved, had his moustache left to grow, so that he might appear before his Captain in the guise of a soldier once more.

CHAPTER VII.

FATHER'S moustache was already long enough for him to pull it between his fingers when one day a two-horse carriage drove up to our farmstead. Two servants sat on the box; they had white gloves on and shiny white coats and white hats with cockades. Our black horse was in the shafts with another, he looked much handsomer now than he used, and he neighed as he came up by the stables. In the carriage sat the Captain and beside him a lady; she had a curling feather in her hat, and in front of it was a dead bird. She came into the parlour; I stood in a corner by the stove and almost bit a hole in my apron with admiration and astonishment. She had a veil with gold stars on it over her face, and when she raised it, oh! how beautiful she was! She threw off her cloak and she had a golden-brown silk dress—

she took off her hat and she had a pale rose-
coloured bow in her hair, and as she stood in
the window and the sun shone on her brown
hair you might have thought it was flaming
fire.

My mother could not say often enough how
happy she was that the lady had come to see
us. The Captain's wife—but she was called the
Baroness in speaking to her—wiped her face
with a fine handkerchief, oh, how that handkerchief was scented! the whole room smelt of
it; she threw open the window and said the
air in the parlour was stuffy; her voice was
something like Cordula's; almost a man's voice.
Mother asked who had played the lady such a
trick as to stick a dead bird in her hat. The
lady laughed, but it was not a frank, pleasant
laugh; she quickly checked it, and said: "My
good woman, it is the fashion."

Mother shrugged her shoulders, then she
called me and said: "Shake hands prettily
with her ladyship."

"Let her be—I cannot bear children; per-

haps because I have none of my own. My
good woman, I am just as plain-spoken as you
country folks are, and if you take it amiss why
you must—I cannot bear children."

This is what the well-bred lady said before
me, and she laughed as she spoke as if it was
something very pleasant and amusing. From
that moment I took a dislike to the lady, such
a bitter grudge that I felt as if I could have
poisoned her. And I loved the Captain himself all the more who drew off his glove and
stroked my cheeks—what a soft delicate hand
it was!

Mother thought no more about the Baroness
not choosing to have anything to do with children; she told her all about my brothers
and sisters who were dead, and showed her
the garlands which hung framed and glazed
on the wall; their names were written fair
inside them with comforting texts of scripture.
Father was complaining to the Captain that
one of his horses was sick and they went together to the stables, then mother showed the

Baroness all over the house, and how many
beds there were; several were of my grandmother's time and perhaps older still.

Oh dear! it was all so full of plenty, and
where is it all gone to?—

Presently, when my parents and the Captain and his wife were seated at our well-spread
board the Captain asked:

"Well, Leontine, and are you converted?"

"How converted?" said my mother.

"Yes, my good friends, I brought my wife
with me that she might for once learn to know
our true high-souled peasantry. Until now she
has been possessed by an aversion and pre-
judice against them; she always fancied that
among them everything was rough and coarse;
now she can see for herself how good and admirable everything is in a high-class well-
managed yeoman's farm.—Certainly, my dear
Leontine, there are few indeed like this."

"Oh! yes — I am converted," said the
Baroness, making a sanctimonious face like a

child coming home from her confirmation, and as she laid her hand with its fine slender fingers on that of my mother, father said:

"Aye—my lady, the conversion is on both sides for my wife too—"

"You never would!"—interrupted my mother apologetically, and her cheeks flamed scarlet as my father went on:

"Aye—my wife always thought that fine folks, who speak just like books, could never be quite honest."

They all grew pleasant together, one laughing at another, and my father, with his moustache, seemed to talk freer than ever. The Captain had no spectacles on that day, and mother asked, whether his eyes had been cured.

"Oh no!" said he, "but my wife will not allow that I have bad eyes."

The Baroness gave her husband a hard spiteful look, and said:

"This good woman here has told me of all her severe sufferings and only see how she bears them. Men, who are so ready to call us weak creatures, cannot bear any pain; in that, we women are much stronger. Take example by this humble farmer's wife; from this day forth you are never to groan and growl any more; I will have no more of it."

She was almost laughing as she spoke and the Captain bit his lip.

When they left, the Baroness once more repeated how much she had been pleased at our place, and she gave her hand to my father and mother, but not to me. When they had driven off and my father was praising the fine lady, my mother said:

"She is a bitter, cruel woman; she never looks you straight in the face."

"She does not squint?"

"No, but she never looks you straight in the face. How she scolded her husband before us! and he could not make a quarrel of it when we were by. Because she is strong and healthy she thinks it a disgrace to be ill. And how meek her good husband is to her, why he lies down for her to walk over. When she seated

herself in the carriage he wrapped her feet in a
rug—I saw, she had gold heels to her shoes—
and he asked her: 'Is that right, my darling?'
and she never even thanked him."

CHAPTER VIII.

FROM that day forth the perfect agreement and unity of my parents were at an end; and I myself was in the first instance the guilty cause of this. The Captain came again and again, and once he said to me that he wanted to make me a present for my confirmation, and I was to wish for something. Mother forbid me to accept any present; the man was no relation of ours, nor yet my godfather, and we were not at all the sort of folks who ought to accept anything. But father said that it was an honour being done me, that people of distinction accepted presents from royal personages, and that he knew certainly much best what was done in the world. I, of course, took my father's view, and when the Captain came again about the delivery of the sleeper-logs, I said I wished for a gold chain—a fine, thin gold chain to go five times round my neck. And I had it, and what was finest of all, it had a clasp and on it was my name 'Brigitta' in raised gold letters. No other child had the fellow to it, and I was even prouder of it than of my fine clothes at my sister's wedding. I was almost angry with my mother for saying: 'A man may be strangled even with a gold chain.' And yet it was very near coming true.

Mother grew more and more dejected and morose, and father more and more gay and merry, and I was gay and merry too. There was always plenty of cash in the house, and ready money is a smiling sight, and my father smiled too as he piled up the gold and silver. Perhaps my mother even did not know where the money came from — I certainly did not. Mother wished him to give it all up, he was not fit for a man of business; she thought he ought to let the forester Jorns know, as he had promised; but father said the government would not run away, and he put off going

to Jorns from month to month. When we
heard say that government had bought a farm-
property higher up, father said: "They must
come to me yet, they cannot pass over me, for
I lie right in their way," and he pointed it out
on a map of the neighbourhood, which the
Captain had given him at some time or other.
Mother said: 'Well it may happen to you as
it did to Aussichtler.' He was a little man
who had always industriously and honestly
earned his living as a clock-case-maker, on a
plot of high ground, and his wife they say, was
the prettiest woman far and near; then there
came to him a number of people who had
measured out the land all round; elegant, fine
ladies came too, and they all said that the
Princess must positively build a country-house
here, for this was the finest view and the best
air in all the country round. From that time
forth the poor little man lost his wits, he
worked no more and was always on the look
out for the people who were to buy his
view. His wife died, and the man thought

that every one who came wanted to buy his view.

As my mother told this about Aussichtler, father struck his fist on the table; then he suddenly burst out laughing and said: "I was a fool to be angry—I have the full use of my senses and shall keep them."

Aye — he always prided himself on being very sharp and clever, and the Captain always persuaded him to believe it.

Father went backwards and forwards and once mother accompanied him, but only once and never again; when she came home she complained that it was just as if the whole world was for sale, and everybody's business was to eat and drink and nothing else. As regarded Bergschinder, whom she had met and who was very good friends with father, they had a sharp discussion. Father said mother was much too simple; he could understand now what a benefactor Schaller might be, who bought up estates and woods and sold fields, so that poor folks could acquire some property.

From that time mother never spoke of the matter again.

My father, who formerly used never to leave the farm for months together, was now rarely at home for three days running, but was always riding and driving about. Formerly he never said a word about his victuals, now nothing he got to eat at home was to his fancy, and mother was so heart-broken about it, that she hardly ever eat anything herself. Formerly we had hardly known of the existence of the country postman, now messengers came with letters and telegrams twice a day sometimes, or even three times. At first, my mother would make the messengers welcome and give them something to eat and drink, as our custom was; but she left this off, for they came too often, we might as well have kept an inn, and father too said that there was no need to serve them with food.

Even when father stayed at home he did not seem really at home; he would walk restlessly up and down the room, open and shut

the window, go in and out of the house
— he always seemed to be expecting something.

In the winter we cut down more wood than
we ever had done before; the folks in the neighbourhood earned a great deal, and Aussichtler
was there too—we were always glad to give him
a chance of making a little money; but we had
a great many strangers from a distance to help
in the work, men from all parts with their
wives and children, who had worked on the
railway in the summer. They lived in our
barns and stables, and many of them were a
wild rough set; our farmstead was like a gypsy-
camp.

All round you heard nothing but the strokes
of axes and the crash of falling trees, and the
trunks were dragged down to the valley over
the snow, hundreds and hundreds of them, by
our own horses; it was going on incessantly
from early morning till late at night, and my
father's lips never parted but to give orders or
make calculations. My mother asked—but very

timidly—how this had come about, whether
Jorns, the forester, had given his consent, and
whether some agreement would not soon be
come to with him.

"Aye," said father. "There is no need now
to ask the forest authorities yet; but they want to
make a law in the provincial council that we
are no longer to be masters of our own property. They may make it! and meanwhile I
am cutting down my forest, and the government must come here all the same and give
me the same price for the bare soil as they
would have had to give for it, forest and all."

He farther explained that after the law was
passed timber would be much dearer, and that
was why he was cutting it down now; for wood
would not spoil by keeping, on the contrary,
would improve.

"Well, be patient with me if I ask simple
questions," answered my mother. "Why could
not you leave the timber standing; it would
remain just as good value and go on growing
into the bargain."

"That is what many people ask, who think
themselves a deal cleverer than you. .By and
bye we shall only be able to cut down just so
much as the green-coats allow by measure; then
those who have a stock in hand will have the
best of it."

Mother was satisfied, and only asked again:

"Do you think the Captain is to be trusted
in everything?"

"Aye—as much as you yourself. A man
may follow him blindfold, for he has his eyes
open. Only be quite easy in your mind and
don't let anyone talk you over."

"You are master," said mother. "I have
nothing to say to it." And that she stuck to.

In the spring there was plenty of money in
the house but my father did not let it lie fallow;
he and the Captain bought a forest in Bavaria
through which the railway must run; the Captain had found out about this, and now they
said the only thing was to wait.

CHAPTER IX.

MY father had bought himself a carriage; mother had never got into it, sometimes Ronymus would drive, but more often my father himself. Sometimes he would even take me with him; it seemed as though he did not like to be left alone. When we drove past the roadmender, breaking stones on the road, he would make as though to pull off his cap, but he only scratched his head behind his ear, and stared at us in astonishment.

By the road that leads high up towards the lake of Constance there is a lonely wayside inn; there the Captain used to meet us and sometimes Schaller came too. He greeted the Captain very humbly and my father very slightly and airily; he paced up and down the room, flourishing his riding whip and often switching it across his high boots. He had a

5*

most respectable appearance, and was stout and comfortable-looking, he was getting on in years but still active, and he had a trick of constantly smacking his mouth as if he had something nice on his tongue. When he saw me, he said to my father:

"So that is your only daughter? I wish I had just such another. Don't marry her off till my son comes back from America, and then she shall be my daughter."

Was not this something like a man? A benefactor? And this was the man mother had spoken slightingly of! Aye, thought I, father understands men much better than mother does.·

Schaller enquired of the innkeeper whether no one had asked for him. "Aye—the man who rolls in money," was the answer, and he went to call a very poor peasant, who was al-ways a hanger-on wherever there was anything to eat or to drink. It was said that he had sold his little property for hard cash—for actual bright thalers—that he had strewed them on the ground and rolled on them. From this he had his name Geldwälzer—but of the money he had not a farthing left.

I did not hear what the men said to each other, but father presently stood up and said: "I am your man; I can find the heft for the axe; I am distantly related to Heckenbauer, and what has to be done I can do."

When the Captain praised father, father's whole face lighted up and he went away. I wanted to go with him but he did not take me, and I had to wait alone in the solitary inn. I went outside the house and sat on the bench, and heard the three men inside laughing and talking loud. As I sat there I saw a great spider squatting in the middle of its web, a fly came up and was caught; he thought of course there was nothing there but air, but there were the filmy threads. The fly flutters but cannot escape; it claws with its feet all round and above, but cannot free itself. The spider, no doubt, has discovered that it has caught something, for the whole thing shakes, and who

knows what its thoughts are—but it keeps quite
still; presently the fly is quiet, the spider comes
down on its rope ladder, and the fly begins to
struggle again; away goes the spider, and waits
and waits till the fly stirs no more; then it
spins a shroud round it, draws it close up, and
sucks it dry. As I sat there on the bench it
suddenly struck me: The Captain or Bergschinder is the spider and my father is the fly.

Just as I was thinking this my father came
up, and with him were Heckenbauer and
Schmaje. I went into the parlour with them.
As soon as we went in Schaller turned Schmaje
out again, crying: "If you don't be off, I will
teach you that a Jew cannot have a finger in
the transfer of property."

Schmaje left, muttering something like a
curse; Schaller laughed—he always closed his
eyes when he laughed—and declared that it
was a famous joke; Schmaje might be gulled
and bullied at any one's pleasure. The men
went into the next room with Heckenbauer,
and I heard them strike hands over some bar-

gain, the matter seemed to be settled. Then they came out again. Schaller put a large document into his breast-pocket and they drank a measure of wine. Geldwälzer drank the most.

It was soon night; our horses were put in, and just as we were going to get in, the Captain came up and said to my father that as he now was partner with Heckenbauer in the business he would discount the dividend and give him hard cash down. But father thanked him and said he was a man who would stand by his word, whether to win or to lose.

We drove off, father whistling his military bugle-calls as we went; suddenly we were stopped short—Schmaje stood in the road. He spoke most urgently to my father, warning him against the band of robbers he had got mixed up with.

"Schaller in particular," he said, "is making a fool of you; he calls you the goat that looks lean and is really full of fatness, and says he will cut you up — stable and all. And the

Captain—he out-captains himself—he is just as bad. Shake yourself free; they are leeches, spiders, that will suck your very heart's blood—"

"Aye," cried I, "spiders!" and what I had seen in the afternoon flashed through my mind.

"There, you hear," said Schmaje. "Your child—your own guileless child says even so."

"And she understands just as much about the business as you do; I must stick by it, even if I am cheated."

"Oh, Xander! my dear good fellow," said Schmaje, and he was almost crying, "oh, Xander, you are an honest man, your father was an honest man, your brother Donatus is an honest man—for these thirty years past I have been constantly in and out of your house. Your child here on earth, and your father who is gone to heaven, bear witness that I have warned you. May I never again see the stars—may I never see my own child again, if I am not speaking the truth. Do you think you are a match for Schaller?

Why, do you know what Schaller has done to you?"

"To me! what?"

"The seven devils might take a lesson from him! Why, to make you tame and abject he has allowed himself to be cheated by you. He has—"

"There—that is enough!" interrupted father, "I never cheat. Look here, what will you take —I will give you a hundred gulden—to repeat what you have just said before Schaller and the Captain?"

"A soldier and a lawyer both at once—they are too many for me," said Schmaje sadly enough. "But at any rate don't call the man Captain any longer. He was degraded and turned out of the army with disgrace and infamy by a Court-Martial."

Without making any farther answer my father whipped up the horse and drove off; I looked back and there was Schmaje standing, his hands uplifted to heaven. We went on, but father did not whistle any more, and I said I was sure that Schmaje meant it well. Father said that for all his warm-hearted ways Schmaje was self-seeking and greedy, and only wanted to make him suspicious and unfriendly because he had had no profit out of the business, and could not bear that others should be favoured. He impressed upon me too that I was not to tell my mother anything of what had passed.

"You are now shrewd enough," said he. "And I will tell you in confidence that I do already intend to be quit of the business and to go on living in the old way again; still I must wind up the great job in Bavaria and two others as well. But say nothing about it all to your mother; she is over-anxious, and she is not quite well either."

In the night mother woke me and scolded me:

"What is it you keep calling out about a spider? There is no spider."

I must have been dreaming of the spider.

CHAPTER X.

A FEW days later the Captain came riding up to our house; usually he had a servant behind him, but to-day he was alone, and in the parlour he told father that he had dismissed his groom for speaking disrespectfully to my father a few day since. I went out of doors; Ronymus was standing on a ladder in front of the barn-door, nailing up a dead vulture. He told me he had shot the vulture the day before just as it had got a yellow-hammer in its claws —but the little bird was already dead. The vulture was nailed up, and when Ronymus had come down to the ground again he said:

"Do you know what I should like? I should like to nail up the Captain just like that. He is a vulture, and your father is the yellow-hammer."

He had scarcely said the words when father

came out with' the Captain and told Ronymus
to saddle the horses, and one for himself too to
ride behind them. Ronymus shook his head,
and father shouted out wrathfully: "What are
you standing there for? Do as I tell you."
But Ronymus did not budge from the spot,
and father shouted to him, so that mother came
to look out of the window—

"Are you deaf? Don't you hear what I
order you?"

"Aye — I hear well enough, but I don't
mean to do it. It is not for yourself that you
want it, and the Devil rides behind that
fellow—he is Captain of the Devil's own body
guard."

Father raised his fist, but the Captain stayed
his arm. Ronymus called out:

"Hit me, Captain—hit me, do—and in a
court of justice it will all come out, and the sort
of man you are."

The Captain laughed and spoke in a whisper
to father, who turned away Ronymus then and

there. When he had mounted his horse, he said again:

"If when I come home you are still here, I will flog you off the premises, and set the dogs after you."

Father trotted off with the Captain; he sat his horse splendidly. Ronymus sat down on the water-trough by the conduit, and that is the only time in his life that I ever saw him cry; then he washed his hands and his eyes, and it was almost laughable, as he said:

"I wash my hands in innocence. Oh! Brigitta, you and your mother don't deserve to be miserable; no—nor your father neither. Oh! If only the Captain had hit me! I ought to have fallen on him so that we might have been brought before a court of justice. What a fool! what a coward I was!"

I asked Ronymus if he had learnt to speak in this way from Schmaje; he was startled at my saying this and owned that he had heard from Schmaje, but from others as well, what sort of man the Captain was.

Ronymus went off; my mother, who was not well and could not leave the parlour, called him to go up to her; but he did not go, he went right away carrying his box with his possessions on a truck; he did not shake hands with me, and he never once looked round.

A few days later in the middle of the week my uncle Donatus came; father was not at home, but mother said he might come in at any time if my uncle would wait; this he agreed to and went all over the farm. When he came back into the parlour again, he said: "Things look very badly here, the servants are the masters." But mother would not allow that it was so, she would have nothing said to father's discredit. My uncle said he had not come to stir up strife; he would rather go away again, and for all he knew my father and mother had the property in common.

"What do you mean by the property in

common?" asked mother, and she put on such a melancholy face as I could never describe, and shivered with cold. She asked me where a door and window had suddenly flown open and such a keen draught was blowing, but everything was shut; from that time it seemed to have settled in her, she was always so.

Uncle was about to leave, and just as he actually had his hand on the door, father came in. He made his brother welcome and asked, what had happened that he came up in the middle of the week. Uncle spoke with much violence against all the business matters and against father's partnership with the Captain.

"Was it Schmaje, who told you about it?"

"Aye—and others as well, Xander, you were never one of the sharpest—"

"And because you are my brother am I to take this from you? I don't happen to want anyone to take care of me."

It was very near being a violent quarrel.

Mother said to my uncle—you could see she forced herself to say it:

"Brother-in-law, you did right and well to come; but now, as my husband is by, I may tell you that he told me that he is minded to be quit of the whole business. And now it is all over, let there be peace, and not strife between two brothers. Stay a bit, Donatus, and dine with us." Uncle stopped, and so far all was well. But mother had made too great an effort, she had to go to bed and she never got up again. She wished to have Bonifacia about her, and she came at once. Mother asked father to take Ronymus into service again and father agreed, but it was too late; Ronymus had already engaged himself as coachman, at Ulm.

Father was very gentle and kind to my mother, and she comforted him so far as she could. Once she sent my father and Bonifacia out of the room; she wanted me alone with her.

"Child," said she, "I have still something on my mind. You had that chain given you by that

man—by the Captain ; but never again as long
as you live let a present be made you by any
human creature. And respect your father; he
is honest, and as good as gold, the rogues have
had an easy job with him. Jorns meant well,
he cannot help it. Oh, our pretty farm—our
forest! Merciful God! only one thing do I ask
of Thee; Merciful God! in my last moments
turn my thoughts from the Captain, that I may
not die cursing him—"

Mother died quite easily. How my father
and I cried for her I cannot tell you.

———

CHAPTER XI.

IT proved that the Captain had in fact been degraded from his rank; but I must continue to call him by his title. After that ride with my father he never came to our farm again; it seems that he used the little scene with Rony-mus as a good opportunity for quarrelling with father; there was nothing more to be got out of us. The why and wherefore of the great law-suit that afterwards arose out of it I do not know, and it never was clear to me. I naturally believed my father, who said he should win it —there could be no doubt of that. He was al-ways cursing the Captain, and yet he had nothing more to do with him, for the Captain sold his suit with all its chances to a stranger, and went to Italy or Paris with his wife.

I had only to soothe and comfort my father, he could not make out how or why he had let himself into all this; he still had enough to live on, and only one child. He meanwhile was always hoping that everything would come right again—to be sure we could not bring mother back from her grave.

One day Schmaje came in and he said to my father that a lawsuit was as easily lost as won, and that if he lost it the bailiffs would stand at the door. For the present father was the master of it all, and so what he wanted was to effect a false sale and to buy all our moveable property—the linen and the beds in the house, and the cattle in the stable; the payment might stand over, and if the lawsuit were won the whole transaction would go for nothing; but we should be utter fools to leave everything to the creditors.

"You have been cheated, why should you be a simpleton too?" ended Schmaje.

"That would be a good joke," said my father.

"That is just what it wouldn't be, and you shall give me just what you like for doing it

—it is for your child's sake, and for your wife's sake."

"There, that will do," said my father, and he went to the door and held it wide open. "Take yourself off."

"I will not go," said Schmaje. "I am not going to be turned out of doors by you; your father, looking down from Heaven, will· not allow it. Your father was a good man, your brother Donatus is a good man—hard, no doubt, but a good—"

"And does that make me a bad man? No, no. If I get my property back I will never trust a living soul again, not even you, Schmaje—"

"For all I care you need not trust me then —but trust me now. There stands your child, your only child; will you let her come to beggary; will you let her—God forbid—your only child stand at a stranger's door and—I don't know what—I will not say what. Child, you are old enough to understand, help me and help your father."

"I would rather die of hunger than cheat anyone," said I. I don't know why I said it, but I did.

Schmaje went out leaving the door ajar, my father shut it. When we were alone father sat silent for a long time, and laid his fist on the table; at last he said:

"The Devil has many messengers, but so has the Almighty, and he sent me this one to say, 'only remain honest and you will gain your lawsuit.'"

It turned out otherwise however, the suit was lost. Our farm was sold by auction under the judgment, it was bought by government, and it was said it was to be restored to the forest. The bailiffs stood at the door, aye, and walked in; all was sold. They came, utter strangers came, and behaved as if they, and not we, were at home there. They wrote down everything, from the lofts to the cellar and stable, and put locks on the cupboards and great seals. We could not even go into most of the rooms. In the parlour one of the bailiffs said to my father: "You

may take your soldier's discharge, that belongs
to you," and when they opened my wardrobe,
they said : "Whatever is your own you can
have to keep. Put that chain into your pocket."
He gave me the gold chain with my name, and
I felt as if it burnt my hand, but I put it in my
pocket.

Another day all the men and women of the
neighbourhood came up, and from much farther
off; Schmaje was there too, he bought five of
our horses, and he never looked at my father.
In the parlour a man sat behind the table, before him was a candle burning and everything
was dragged in—beds and linen, all that was
not a fixture was put up to auction, and when
it was knocked down he rapped on the table
with a hammer.

Bonifacia had come and wanted to take me
away with her, but I would not leave father; I
sat with him on the bench by the stove and we
looked on.   I often passed my hand over my
eyes—surely it must be all a dream.   But it
was all real.   The strange men were there, our

goods belonged to them, they carried them off and laughed as they did it. When the pictures of my brothers and sisters with the little memorials of them were taken down and the auctioneer said the pictures were worth nothing, but the frames were, I could not help crying out loud. No one bid for them but Bonifacia; the auctioneer handed them to her, and she said she would take care of them for me.

Then my father's discharge was taken from the wall; the auctioneer took out the paper, and said:

"Xander, the paper belongs to you, but the frame goes with the rest of the things." Father stood up, took the paper out of his hand, and held it in the candle till it caught.

"His name is there," said he. "The Captain ought to be burnt in like manner."

Then he quitted the house. I followed him; he walked on with one hand clasped round his neck, and when I took his other hand, he said:

"That is well, that is right, we will stick by one another."

We did not go into the house again till all the folks were gone. Bonifacia came and begged us to go with her, but father said he would go to his brother and be a servant under him, he still was his brother and his house was their father's house; certainly Donatus ought to have come to fetch him, but he could no longer afford to be proud. Bonifacia had to go home to her husband, I remained alone with my father in our despoiled house; our home was among strangers.

CHAPTER XII.

IT was now night; we took each other's hand, and set out; I told father we must be firm and stout-hearted and neither look back nor think of the past; but he did not answer me and only pressed my hand, then he let go of it. From that moment I perceived that every man must stand upright by himself, and I believe I have acted on that. The dog followed us, but my father drove him away, saying: "I have not even food now."

We went through the wood which was no longer a wood — nothing but thousands and thousands of stumps, and everywhere ravens sitting on them, you never would have thought there were so many ravens at our place. The sun went down and the ravens flew up and croaked.

"He cannot reproach me," said my father.

"No one has any right to do that but you. Oh,
I do not want to go to him! rather would I beg
from door to door, and you can say: This is
my father who once was a proud peasant-owner
with hundreds and hundreds of acres of forest,
and now he has nothing but the beggar's staff
in his hand. Oh, child, I had grown old, so old,
fifty years old was I, when I learned that there
were vile and perjured men in the world."

I comforted my father as well as I could,
but father only said: "I shall never smoke
again." ·

We went on, it was still a long way to my
uncle's; suddenly a keen wind began to blow,
and my father said: "Wind, what do you want
of me? Find the Captain, lift him from the
ground, let him struggle and writhe a bit, and
then tear him into a thousand pieces."

The wind blew his hat off. "Take my head
with it," said he, and he laughed. We hunted
for the hat but could not find it, and father
went on bare-headed; he would not let me
tie a handkerchief round his head, he said,

he had made a way for the wind to blow through it.

We heard the dogs barking in the distant farms.

"They are all barking at me; so long as my trees were standing you could not hear the dogs barking."

My heart quaked within me, and I was thankful when at last we saw the light in my uncle's house. We went towards it; the dogs barked, a window was thrown open, and my uncle asked: "Who is there?"

"I am here, I want to be let into my father's house."

"Your father's house; it is no longer yours; but come up though it is mine."

"Come down and fetch me in."

"You may wait long enough for that."

"Come away—come away," said father to me, and he almost knocked me over.

We turned to go down into the valley again

I did not dare to speak a word to father, and indeed he said:

"Don't talk, not a word. Down there my parents lie buried; they will as soon rise from their graves and go into their own house as I will ever cross that threshold again."

We walked and walked, and how many things I thought of. It came into my mind— in my utter misery it returned to my mind— how once I had been called the Princess of Schlehenhof; I could hear the music at my sister's wedding, and the bugle-call, and my only wish at that moment was that I might some day be revenged on the man who had ruined us.

At last we came to our own village and there we sat, out in the open air, till day broke. We counted the hours as they struck in the tower; there lay my mother and my sister in their graves! Thank God that they had not lived to see this misery.

There, in the houses, the folks lie sleeping, there are so many well furnished beds — the peasants' wives are proud of them—and no one to say to us: 'Come in and be warm and rest.' No one thinks that here outside sit two forlorn and abandoned souls. Oh, the world is hard-hearted!

But no, there were human beings who were thinking of us.

Father had just said: "I am so cold—I wish I was cold once for all." And we heard a voice crying out: "Thank God! I have found you at last."

It was the road-mender coming down from the hill-side in his old soldier's cloak; he hastily drew his flask of Gentian-cordial out of his pocket, saying:

"Drink first, as the farmer said when he was thinking of what he had to do in the city. That's right, drink—another sup. For once in her life Bonifacia was right when she would not let me rest till I got up before daybreak, and went up to Donatus to see how you are getting on. Aye — I should not care to be Donatus — but we will not stop to talk now, come home with me."

And we went with the road-mender.

CHAPTER XIII.

OH! merciful God! there is still refuge and shelter in the world; kind hearts and a warm hearth.

The road-mender and Bonifacia took us in, receiving us as if we were the rich folk of yore and only come to do them the honour of a visit. Bonifacia made a bowl of porridge for breakfast and let me help her, she laid the table with a clean cloth, gave my father the only straw-bottomed chair that was in the room, and brought a silver spoon out of her cupboard saying: "That was your christening present to Ronymus."

"I can eat with a pewter spoon and must be thankful for what is in it," answered my father, and he laid the spoon on the table; he felt it hard to owe a bowl of porridge to the kindness of such humble folks, but he forced himself to eat and a tear fell into the first spoonful of the porridge he had ever had given to him—But that was the last tear he ever shed, from that time forth.

When he had eaten he was fain to tell about his brother Donatus; the road-mender wanted him to wait awhile, but father would not give in, and when he had ended, he said: "What do you say to that, man?" The road-mender shrugged his shoulders.

"Well, it is not right," he said, "but still you have done your brother some injury; it is not a small matter to an honourable and proud peasant that he should have a brother, who has —well, to speak mildly, who has muddled his affairs."

My father sighed. "Aye, aye," said he, "I must let myself be lectured by anyone now-a-days—But I can take it patiently from you, you mean it kindly."

Father wanted to go out at once with the road-mender, and help him to break stones, but the road-mender put him off and said, father must consider a bit, and when father said he had considered and he should stick to it, the man shook his head.

"Nay, don't do it—not yet. I have a parti‑ cular reason. Do you know what is hardest to bear in addition when a man has fallen . into misery?"

"A bad conscience."

"Well, that of course; but for that every man can be his own physician and his own apothecary. I meant something else than that: to be sick in poverty is what I mean. Don't let yourself fall ill, you must keep well now. Go to bed—another day will dawn after this, and then you can do what you like, if you want my advice I shall be here and ready."

A gleam like a faint ray of sunshine passed over my father's melancholy face; he let him‑ self be put to bed by the road-mender like a little child, and very soon the man came back into the parlour and said: "He is asleep." Then he went out to his work, taking Aussichtler with him, for he lived in the house too, and was al‑

ways blowing into a clarinette. I felt in my pocket and sure enough I had lost the chain the Captain had given me. I know for certain that I put it in my pocket; I must have lost it when I wanted to tie a handkerchief round father's head. It was best so. I wanted no memorial of the Captain; I wished we could lose all recollection of him.

About midday father woke up and was quite fresh again; he made the road-mender give him a cap and a heavy hammer and went out with him on the road, and helped to break the stones. In the evening father said to him:

"Tell me everything, what do folks say and think of me?"

"What does it matter? Besides I don't know what other folks say and think. For God's sake don't be thin-skinned. Nothing can be more stupid than to make a show of your troubles to other folks; they have no time for such things and are only provoked with

those who get into trouble if they are not
downright spitefully glad—"

"But you yourself, what do you think?
Speak it out; you mean it kindly, and I will
take anything from you."

"I don't know that it will help you much.
First tell me, whom do you yourself consider to
blame, yourself or others?"

"Both."

"Aye, that is just how it is, and of course
you lay the least blame on your own shoulders.
I don't say you were a simpleton—on the contrary, too sharp. In one word, the devil at the
bottom was greed. Here is a peasant who
lives like a king on his own property, and he
must need take to business, and why? He has
got a good estate with his wife and he is proud,
he thinks he must earn a fortune to match for
himself. For a long time he has hardly confessed it to himself till one day a crafty meddler
comes to him and puts it into words, and he
feels as if he were suddenly waked up from
sleep—"

"That's it, just so!" cried my father. "But how did you know all that?"

"How? the birds by the highway chirruped it to me. From that time forth your one word was, to scrape, and save, and take advantage. You thought no one could take you in; it was not that you were stupid but just not clever enough for your companions, especially the Captain."

"But you have not anything good to say of him, surely?"

"No—I could crack him over the skull with my hammer — he deserves the worst he can get."

"And don't you believe that he will get it yet?"

"What a man's lot may be no man can foretell, any more than the weather to-morrow. As to his troubling himself about you? Nay, the man who can turn thief never troubles himself to think any farther how those he has robbed may fare."

The road-mender was very careful what he

said, and my father took all he said in good
part because he was just as furious against the
Captain as we were ourselves.

Five human souls sat round the board in the
little cottage outside the village; and the fare
was only potatoes and porridge, porridge and
potatoes day after day, year in and year out,
but contentment gave it salt and savour. Father
broke stones now on the highway where we had
driven in our own carriage and where our eight
good horses had dragged our own timber; the
men as they passed on their way to the fields
would stop a while, and many would come
past that way on purpose to stare at the head-
peasant of Schlehhof, but he never cared about it.

At first to be sure he confessed to me that
he never believed that his brother would leave
him there, and that the other peasant-owners
would not have done so either, that they would
be sure to come and fetch him away and help
him on to his feet again. But when day after
day went by, and no one came near us, he said,
'well, it was all one to him; he was only glad

that he could still work enough to earn his
daily food.' Still he found it hard to accustom
himself to poverty; the first time he had to put
on wooden shoes, he said:

"Sometimes I feel as if it were not all in
earnest—as if the Almighty were playing me
some scurvy joke; but God Almighty is no
jester. In my dreams almost every night I
strike the Captain dead, in all sorts of different
ways, and then I am dragged before the judge;
when I wake up I am thankful to find that I
may still go stone-breaking. But I should just
like to know how the Captain contrives to be
able to sleep."

Whenever we thought of the Captain it
seemed to renew all our misery.

Father was never afraid of any weather, and
he never complained about it, but he was often
put out by the wind. A thing that went to his
heart was every Sunday when he had to go to
church and might not sit in the seats kept for
the village council, but had to stand with the
poor folks. But once as I was going home with

him—the road-mender's cottage was our home now—he said:

"It ought not to be—there ought to be no seat of honour in a church, we are all equals before God."

I helped father too to break stones, but after a few days he would not allow me to go on; he would not have the disgrace attach to him that he could not earn a living for his only child. And I had to obey him, for he threatened if I did not, to go into Alsace and work in a factory, and when he said that I gave in to him in everything.

CHAPTER XIV.

AUSSICHTLER was a most extraordinary
man, just a careless merry musician. He was
quite content to make music for his own pleasure, and equally content that it should give
pleasure to others, but if there was no one to
hear him it was all one to him. If he had
wherewith to live for a few days—and the good
people did for him very cheaply—he was perfectly happy, and had no care for anything
beyond. He had formerly been a wood-carver
too, and often did a little work in that way; I
learnt, from him, to carve in wood too, and we
made sheep and cows and little dolls, quite
coarse work, but it found a sale and brought in
some small earnings. Aussichtler went round
with them to sell or took them to market when
he could get nothing by his music. Bonifacia
kept everything in good order, I earned enough

for us to be able to buy a goat between us, and we had five cocks and hens and three geese too belonging to us; and could you believe it? when the men were out at work, and we had done the work of the house and sat together in the parlour, we used to sing as if all the world were happy and everything were right, and as it should be.

Uncle Donatus once sent father word that he would pay his passage if he would go to America. What answer my father sent I don't know, but it was nothing pleasant, I am very certain. My cousins, Donatus' children, often passed by the house, but they always behaved 'as if they did not know me, and so I did not know them.

As long as we were rich the whole neighbourhood had been like one little paradise of affectionate relatives; now my father and mother might have sprung from the rock. Certainly it was particularly unlucky that all our connexions had lost money through father, for the Captain and the others had found out wherever

there was any one related to us, and had
bought and borrowed, and remained in their
debt.

I succeeded in making my father smoke
again, for my sake, and we were very well content; I had to lengthen my dresses again and
again, I grew so tall in the two years we were
at the road-mender's; till that time I had been
little. In the winter evenings father and the
road-mender made wooden shingles.* Once he
suddenly lifted his knife high in the air, and
said: "I should like to drive that into
the Captain's breast, and turn it round seven
times."

We were greatly startled—father still thought
thus of the Captain! but we said nothing further,
no more did he.

One day Ronymus came home for a day's
leave; he was a soldier. Father was the first
to give him his hand, and say he had been
right to speak so to the Captain. Ronymus
was quite respectful to father, and he saw that

* The houses being roofed with wood.

I was grateful to him for this; but he could not
wonder enough at my having grown so tall—
taller almost than he was. "You are the head-
peasant's daughter—every inch of you," he said,
but that was all.

It was in the second spring; the sun was
shining brightly and we had hung out the
washing—when I saw my father laugh once more
as heartily as ever. Our three geese had gone
off the day before and we did not know
where; we hunted for them till midnight and
could find them nowhere; now we suddenly
heard them snapping their beaks just in front
of the house. Bonifacia ran into the sitting-
room where the men were just going out, crying out: "Here are our geese!" and I ran after
her calling out too: "Our geese are here, God
be praised and thanked, our geese again!" At
the same time the geese gobbled and cackled
as if they wanted to tell us where they had
been all night, and their clatter and our out-
cries made my father laugh till the tears ran
down his cheeks, and he had to sit down. At

last he said, and he could hardly speak for laughing: "You have each of you three half-geese—well, well, how funny! And one may be thankful and joyful over three half-geese."

That was the last time my father laughed.

———

CHAPTER XV.

AYE, it was spring again, and in spring one always feels as if something special had been bestowed on one. But in truth we were well off and might well be content. Bonifacia and I gardened together in the little patch of ground that belonged to the cottage; it was but small to be sure, but in the course of the summer we turned the ground over three and four times, planting something fresh each time, all sorts of things needed in the house, and everything throve for us. Our goat had a kid too and our hens had begun to lay, so we had milk and eggs in the house, and Bonifacia always cooked more and better for my father than for her husband. He indeed did not look askance at his food but was pleased with everything, and Bonifacia was always just the same as when she was maid-servant in our own house.

But father always looked gloomy, and if
any one noticed it he would shrink away, no
one dared say anything to him; he declared he
should be quite calm and contented whatever
might be required of him, and he eat and drank
and slept just as he used, but he hardly ever
spoke at all.

I learnt afterwards that he had once met
my uncle Donatus, and that the brothers had
passed each other without a greeting as if they
did not know each other. When they were
passed father stood still a bit, waiting in case
his brother should call to him, but he went on
his way.

Father was one day out on the highroad at
some distance from the road-mender, breaking
stones with his big hammer, when some old
beams and rafters, all brown with smoke, were
carted past. Father asked where they came
from, and was told that the barns had been
pulled down, and that to-day the house was
being pulled down up at Schlehenhof. What
came over my father then, who can tell? He

flung the great hammer into the middle of the
road and ran off straight away to Schlehenhof.
Aussichtler met him in the forest and called to
him, but father shook his head and ran on; he
shouted something, but Aussichtler could not
hear what.

Father got up to our house where they were
just beginning to tear down the front-gable with
fire-hooks; he sprang through the fire-hooks,
grasped the side posts of the front doorway and
screamed out: "My farm! my house! my wife!
Captain—"

The men flung away their tools and tried
to get at father, but it was too late, the gable
came hurling down; there was a crash, one last
shriek—and the men shrieked too—then silence
—only a beam rolling down on the top of the
others. Father was dead—

Well—I lived through it. What is there
we cannot live through? but I cannot tell you
what I felt when they brought father down on
a timber-truck. An empty sack was spread
over his head and it had his name on it! I

wanted to raise the sack, but the folks held me
back, and said I had better not see him, his
face was so fearfully disfigured.

My uncle was at the funeral, and afterwards
came to me in the parlour. When he saw the
frames on the walls with the wreaths and the
names of my dead brothers and sisters he said,
it was well for them that they had died young;
then he said I could go to him if I chose. I
did not answer him. I heard everything and
saw with my eyes wide open, but I felt as if I
were only half awake, as if I had had a blow
with a heavy hammer on the top of my head. I
heard them whisper one to another, 'Brigitta may
be going mad, she looks already like a mad
woman, and she has not shed a single tear
yet.' I heard it, and I could not say a
word, I was like a person who is walled-up
alive.

Bonifacia spoke to me as none but such a
good soul can; the priest too told me affection-
ately how I might comfort myself, for I had
always been a good daughter and that death

was indeed a release for my father. I could say nothing to it all but "I must wait." I felt as if something might come—I did not know what, that would help me and cure me, that would cool my head and rouse me up and tell me why I must live through all this.

I worked in the garden as on other days; the sun shone brightly, the birds were piping, but it was for others, it had nothing to do with me; I felt myself as if I were mad; I saw and heard everything, and could not realise it or care for anything. On the second day after the funeral suddenly at noon I felt so tired that I could hardly drag myself to my bed. Bonifacia undressed me like a little child and lifted me into bed and there I slept, as Bonifacia told me, without turning from that noon till the next morning; Bonifacia never left my bed-side.

I woke up, and when I saw my father's clothes hanging on the wall the tears at last burst forth, and Bonifacia said:

"Aye—only cry a bit. Thank God that you

can cry; now all will be well." She dried my
tears, but they flowed again and as if they never
would cease. When at last I said I was so
desperately hungry she was perfectly happy. I
got up and dressed myself, I eat and drank,
and then it was that it was fully borne in upon
me that I must trust to myself, and hold myself bravely upright and not let my life sicken
and pine, who could tell what might happen to
me yet.

Aye—from that hour I took heart and found
fresh courage, and I never lost it again, but one
single time, and that too is gone and overpast.

CHAPTER XVI.

I COULD not stay any longer with the road-mender. There was something waiting for me to do out in the world, what it was I did not know, but I must go. I belonged to nobody now, and had no one but myself to look to.

These were my thoughts for many days, and many times I spoke aloud to myself so that Bonifacia said: "Whom are you speaking to?" I wanted to be off and yet could not go; it was like when a man lies awake in the morning, and says to himself, 'You must get up' and yet lies there. I wanted something to tear me away.

The host of the lonely inn up on the hill, where that band of robbers used to meet, came in one day and asked me if I would take service with him, and with a mean leer, half smiling and half sorrowful, he added that his wife

8*

might die before long, and then I might be
mistress of the inn. What I said I have now
forgotten, but when the innkeeper was gone
Bonifacia said: "You can let fly with your
tongue bravely; I never should have thought
it of you."

It was clear to me now that the well-to-do
always take advantage of the poor and forsaken
and are impudent to them too. But I would
soon show them the stuff I was made of. I
could not rest any more, I must be off and
away and prove what the world had in store
for me.

It was not an easy matter to me to bid
farewell to the road-mender's cottage. Bonifacia went with me part of the way, and out
on the road her husband gave me his hand and
said: "Ask at the barracks for Ronymus, and
don't be a bit afraid; he may be of use in many
ways." He said no more; we went onwards,
and soon heard him breaking stones again. We
went up the hill, and Bonifacia said: "Don't

go into the church-yard now; you must not fret
yourself for nothing, you can do the dead no
good by it and you want all your strength.
Pray for them in silence and I will do the same
for you."

We went a little way farther without speaking, and up by the forest Bonifacia took my
hand in both hers, and broke into sobs as she
said: "The storm of misfortune has spent itself;
now things will go well with you. Depend
upon that and always remember that when all
else fails, you still have a home with us. So
long as I live, or my husband, we will honour the
graves of those who belonged to you, and I will
keep the portraits of your brothers and sisters for
you till you have a house of your own, and you can
have your share of the goat and the geese and
the poultry whenever you want it. God bless
you and keep you straight." She turned away,
stood for a moment and called once more:
"Remember me to Ronymus too."

'Remember me to Ronymus,' those were the
last words I heard then from Bonifacia, and

quite involuntarily the words set themselves to all sorts of tunes and yet I did not want to sing. I was in no mood for that.

I walked on, seeing nothing of wood and field, it all swam before my eyes. I sat down on a rock, for I was as tired as if I had already walked miles. I eat the last scrap of bread that Bonifacia had stuffed into my pocket; a little bird perched not far from me and let me feed it; when I had nothing left it flew away.

Down in the hollow trickles the brook that flows on for ever day and night, to-day as it did yesterday, whether men live or die, whether anyone sees it or not. There lie ruined heaps of rock on which young fir trees are beginning to grow; my fingers pull tiny mosses from the stone, and as I look at the plants I cannot help recalling how the school-teacher told us once that it takes hundreds and hundreds of years before anything can cling to the rock, and then hundreds and hundreds more before a grain of seed can take root and a shrub grow

up on it. And men can cut them down so
quickly! Why do we run about in the world,
and make our lives a vain weariness and
trouble? I want nothing but to die now, at
once—

In that hour, when I was lonely and forsaken I truly found God. I had always gone
to church and to Communion as was the custom; but it was then, in solitude and abandon-
ment, that I first truly felt that I was not alone
and forsaken in the world, that God was with
me, that he held me by the hand and would not
let me fall. The whole world seemed to become as
light a matter as a game for children, only one
must play too and not stand aside; I could not
let myself be set in a corner, I had my share
in it and belonged to it too.

I looked down on our village; I should have
liked to go down and have said to everybody:
"Don't you know that we are not mere lost
children?" but what good would that do; they
would say, 'Aye—they knew it.' I had felt so
before, but this was the first time I knew it by

experience as surely as it is daylight now; and
that knowledge never left me and never will
leave me. But I do not care to talk about it
in general; it is a thing to have and keep to
oneself.

My weariness was gone; I felt as if I had
fallen asleep in eternity and should never need
to rest or sleep any more. I stood up, feeling
as if I could fly; I heard the geese clattering in
the village, and it seemed as if I heard them
over head where the lark sings. Then I heard
the clarinette out of the window in the roof of
the cottage; since my father's death till now
Aussichtler had never played any music; now
he was playing—and what? The burden of the
song:

> "The cherries they be black and red,
> And I'll love my love till I be dead."

How long it was since I had sung that and
met the Captain! It must have been some one
else that had sung and done that, and not I.

But it is well and necessary that we should

now and then look back and reflect on the
world and on ourselves.

I crossed the hill and came out upon the
high-road. The weather had changed suddenly;
a cold rain fell in my face, a keen wind had
risen, and the earth was so slippery that I went
sliding at every step; but I walked steadily forwards, I was healthy and not a coddle, and I
was as warm as if I had been drinking hot
wine.

As I walked straight on I heard a timber
waggon; I felt as if I heard for the first time
how it creaked and bumped on the road, and
how the stones crunched, and the drag under
the wheel ground and scraped the earth.

I stood still, the cart came nearer, the driver
was Sepper with his red waistcoat and his red
face; the horses drawing it had been our own,
and the brown beams had come from our house.
Sepper told me he was carrying them to
the town; that turners and wood-carvers were
glad to get it, that such old wood was not to
be had now; he invited me to get up and ride

with the bundle I carried, and I rode to the town on the beams out of our own house.

Sepper spoke but little, and that suited me best; only once he said: "The farm was forest once, and now it will become forest again." Just by the Bridge the man had to unload; I got down and went on into the town. There the folks were going to and fro, each knowing whither—I only knew not where I was going. Men and women came out of the factories; many were laughing but they did not look gay. I had kept my father from this—an old peasant owner turned factory-hand, that would never do — but if all else failed I must learn this work; still this was the last thing I would try.

I went into the Cathedral; there I was as much at home as anyone else; that belonged to no one, and no one could turn me out. I sat and knelt there a long time; I had no prayer-book but I needed none; I knew all I wanted to say. I came out of the church, and I had lived so utterly out of the world that it struck me as quite strange to see the women sitting in the market-place—it was market-day—and offering all kinds of goods for sale. A heavy waggon loaded with sacks of corn came out of the corn-exchange; who was the man walking by the cart? Yes—it was he; none other than my brother-in-law, the husband of my sister who died. I called his name, he stood still and looked round; I signed to him and leaped over the baskets round me so that the women scolded again; I was soon standing by his side and he gave me his hand.

———

CHAPTER XVII.

"I MIGHT have met you a hundred times, and I should never have known you, you are so altered—so tall and so—but you cannot have got a new pair of eyes, and I did not think you had such eyes."

So said my brother-in-law, and he could not get over his astonishment. He wanted to fetch witnesses out of the market-hall that he had let me know through the farmers of the neighbourhood that I might live with him if I did not know where else to go. I needed no witnesses, I took his word for it; he had always been a good kind man, and as to what happened later he could not help it, he meant well.

Of course I asked first after Agnes, my sister's child. My brother-in-law must have seen by my face how glad I was still to have some one belonging to me. He said: "You need not tell me anything, I know all. It is a bargain—you come with me. My wife said—you will soon see for yourself that she is a kind soul—as soon as we heard of your misfortunes: 'Now you ought to fetch your sister-in-law, and take her into the house'—You will come with me?"

"Aye, that I will."

Oh! how delightful this was. I loved his wife already, and I must say she deserved it. At the inn, where I had a meal with my brother-in-law, he said to me:

"Brigitta, I lost a good bit of money too through your father—but that is no business of yours; he was an honest man for all that, and had to atone for his over-confidence in a scoundrel. Where is *he* now? you don't know? So much the better, we don't want him. Now be happy. You will like it very much down with us, and if Agnes has lost one mother she now has two instead."

I went on with my brother-in-law, and on

the way there was a good deal of joking, for folks thought I was his wife, and he always spoke to me directly as 'sister-in-law.' But I told him that at home I would not be called so, that I would serve him honestly as a servant, and my perquisites would be the privilege of living with my own sister's child. Even on the road home I saw that my brother-in-law had become quite another man since he had been in Switzerland—so wide-awake and clever, I never thought he had it in him. We crossed the Lake of Constance; the Swiss mountains look quite different when you are close to them to what I had seen from home, but I paid no particular heed to them then; when your heart is as full as mine was, it is all the same where you are.

There was no railway then, and my brother-in-law's light cart was waiting for us at the landing-place at Rorschach. We drove through a beautiful country, and my brother-in-law, who had become a thorough Swiss, was proud of its beauty.

We arrived at Rheinfeld and his wife said as she welcomed me:

"You are like your father, in face and figure, only your _eyes are different," folks always noticed my eyes.—"We had a great regard and esteem for him, and he had to pay heavily for fancying himself a man of business when he was nothing of the kind; but he was a good honest man."

Oh! I was at home! no work could be too hard for me where they spoke so of my father. I could have kissed the woman's hands. Beyond this she did not say many words to me, it is not the way with the Swiss; but she always remained sincere and kind, and the same one day as another.

When Agnes came in from school, her stepmother said to her:

"Come—give your little hand, this is your Auntie."

But the child did not come up to me, and the mother would have been angry with her, but I said in a whisper:

"Don't take it ill in the child. What does a child understand when it is told, 'This is your aunt, you must be fond of her?' It will soon come when she sees I am fond of her."

As I said this the mother gave me her hand once more.

"You are right," said she. "The child will soon perceive that you are blood relations. Blood is thicker than water." My sister-in-law and I became the best of friends from the very first hour.

My brother-in-law still kept an inn; there is nothing more advantageous to an inn-keeper than to have his own belongings in the house so that there is no petty stealing, and I saw that I was of use. My sister's child, little Agnes, was all to me that I looked to her to be; she loved me dearly and the other children used to be jealous because she often would say I was her Auntie only and not theirs. I was quite satisfied and contented about her, her step-

mother was very good to her—but a child can
never have love enough.

For two years I lived a peaceful and honourable life with my brother-in-law. A man who
was particularly friendly to me, was a colonel
who lived at Sträussle; he was an old soldier
formerly in the papal army, who almost all the
year round had a fresh flower for his button
hole and a little glass tube below with water in
it to keep the flowers fresh. He had always
praised me highly, and one day he told me
privately that I might make my fortune, that
a rich fruit merchant in Rorschach, who was in
partnership with my brother-in-law, had his eye
on me. I had often seen this man and spoken
to him; he was very respectable, not yet old,
and very friendly to me, but I had never
troubled myself about that; a great many men
had been friendly to me, but no one had ever
presumed upon that. Of course I often had to let
folks tell me to my face that I was pretty—that
was the reason I served in an inn—and folks like
to amuse themselves by flattering a girl in that

way; but every one knew that they dared not come any nearer than that.

One day the Colonel was there and with him the fruit-merchant; they were dressed in their Sunday-best and talking privately to my brother-in-law. Then the fruit-merchant came straight up to me, and said:

"By the way you behave to little Agnes I see you would be a good step-mother—I am a widower and I have two children."

I did not find it easy to say 'no' to the good man; he listened quietly and only asked me—and he looked so tenderly kind as he spoke—whether I would not consider of it, and I had to say that I had already considered. He gave me his hand and spoke never another word, but went away.

I don't think that it was pride, I only felt that I could not consent.

From that day forth my brother-in-law became, I cannot say unkind, but still no longer kind to me; he told me I had thrown away my chance, and that after what had happened in my family I ought to have been glad to get into such a respectable house. This hurt and grieved me.

Not long after an exchange was made with some people in the Pays de Vaud; Agnes was sent there to learn French and we had a child from the Pays de Vaud. I was not asked my opinion; Agnes' departure broke a piece of my heart away, and from that time forward I could never feel the house my home.

I was with my brother-in-law two years and a half; then I went into service at Heyden up yonder at the inn at Freihof; I was head of the house belonging to the inn — a sort of annexe—and had the management of everything. When I left, my brother-in-law was quite kind again, and his wife still more so. Indeed she had always been just the same; and I believe she never knew that my father's life and death had been made a reproach to me.

CHAPTER XVIII.

Now I was for the first time really and truly a servant, for though I had served at my brother-in-law's place still I was his sister-in-law.

Nothing can be more vexatious than when servants try to lord it over each other; however up at Freihof there was nothing of that sort. The inn-mistress — who was the widow of a Colonel—was always first and foremost in all the work, and her daughter was the same; there was no preference or favour, and the servants never tried to domineer one over another so as to vex each other. May be that that is the free sturdy nature of the Swiss; for here, in my own country, I have had great difficulty in getting my own servants to see the sense of it.

Well—I was a servant and was very willing to serve. Up on the high ground I felt as light and free as if I were only a visitor for fresh air during the summer; and as for work —there was plenty of it, but I was willing to work. Upstairs and downstairs I was always singing as if I expected some good fortune to come to me the next morning—nay the very next hour.

I had many guests, single visitors or whole families; but I was always told that the gay world and busy time did not come till the great Doctor arrived from Berlin. A whole herd of people preceded him, who had complaints in their eyes and who settled with us, or in the village or neighbourhood, and awaited his coming.

He came, and the first time I ever saw him I felt at once that this was the good fortune, the happy presentiment, that hovered over me. I put a nosegay in his room for him; I would have strewed flowers in his path wherever he went. And as I felt at the first moment, so

I did always, and he must no doubt have seen how I felt towards him.

I brought him some water — I should have been ready to wash the feet he stood on.

"What is your name?" he asked—and what a voice he had!

"Brigitta," said I, "but I am mostly called 'Gitta,' and please, speak to me as if I were no stranger."

"Are you related to the people here?"

"No, I come from the Black Forest."

"Have you any parents?"

"No."

"Nor brothers and sisters?"

"No."

I could not but look at him as he asked these questions, surely he must know all about me, he who knew everything in the world, from whom nothing was hidden.

The doctor had a look—I cannot tell you— so full of a saintly melancholy and at the same time so inspiriting — wherever he went he

brought healing with his mere presence, and his
voice lulled sorrow to rest; the most impatient
and rebellious got better and turned meek with
him. From every part the pilgrims came; it was
quite different to what it had been down at Ein-
siedeln. Men, women and children came, rich and
poor—it was all the same to him. He came up
into the mountains to get some rest, but men such
as he are never allowed to rest. When he went out
walking I used to thank God that now for once
he could be by himself and breathe in peace;
but they would lie in wait for him by the way
and would run after him, and he never was
put out by them. And such a man as that
must die!

Upstairs in my room hangs his portrait with
his own signature. But what can be said of a
portrait? His look and the tone of his voice
cannot be put on to the paper. But at that
time he was still young and active, and had not
a white hair in his beard.

Among the patients who waited for the
Doctor was an Englishwoman from India with

a wonderfully pretty little girl named Seridja; she had ruddy golden hair, and a face like milk and blood, but she was a downright little devil, whose chief delight it was to torment the people round her. This child was blind, and she ill-used everyone that came near her; she treated her mother like a servant and her maid like a dog. This maid, a good-hearted Indian woman, had been her wet-nurse, she was called Baboo, and the child never had a kind word either for her mother or her nurse.

Now when the Doctor first examined Seridja's eyes she screamed and fought like one possessed; she was the only patient that had ever been refractory under his hand, nor soothed by the sound of his voice; he sent away both mother and child, and said there was nothing to be done at least for a year.

But he performed several great cures. I used to let the folks he had cured tell me all about it, and joined them in praising God and blessing the man. I was as happy as if I had

never known sorrow in my life; trouble came
upon me again however, but, thank God, it was
only a passing squall.

One day I was standing outside arranging
some washing, and singing softly to myself.
The sky was so blue, the air so fresh and sweet
up on the hills, there you live as free and blithe
as a bird; for a minute or more I had the feeling that I hardly knew what I was or where I
was. Something startled me; I heard the
Doctor's voice at the lower house that was the
hotel itself. I went to the gallery; there stood
the doctor in front of a carriage loaded with
trunks, saying:

"Have patience, Baron — it is not possible to decide or to make any experiment as
yet."

In the carriage sat a man and a lady, and
who were they? —— The Captain and his
wife. I had to hold myself up by the rail-
ings.

The postillion blows his horn, the carriage
drives off, close by me; I had not been mis-

taken, it was the Captain and his wife, and a handsome young man was sitting with them. I had to collect myself to remember where I was, all the world seemed turning round me. I tried to count the linen, but I could not even count properly, I was quite dazed.

'Merciful God, do what you will with me, only never let me set eyes on that man again!'

So I thought to myself, and just then I heard Bonifacia's voice. I thought it could not be true — but it was true. Bonifacia had come with her husband, who had one eye tied up; a splinter of stone had flown into his eye, and he was suffering great pain. I told him that if there was anyone in the world who could help him, it was the great eye-doctor.

Bonifacia answered that was just what Ronymus had said. Ronymus had served his time as soldier and was a house-servant now at Basle; the great Doctor had passed a night there, and Ronymus had sent the money home for his father to make the journey to see him.

"He is a real good son," said Bonifacia. "And how pleased he will be to hear that we have come upon you up here."

How glad we all three were to meet I need not tell you. It was a relief to my heart to have those near and dear to me at hand so as to tell them that I had seen the Captain again, though only for an instant.

"And I have brought you a remembrance of the Captain," said the road-mender. "See, here is your chain with your name on it. Some children who were picking berries in the wood found it. I brought it with me, meaning to take it to your brother-in-law."

I held the chain in my hand once more, and as I looked at it, that night rose up in my mind when I walked with father through the wood down to my uncle's. Why had it all come back to me, why was it not all past and forgotten for ever?

However, this was no time for following up such thoughts.

CHAPTER XIX.

I WENT to the Doctor and told him that my best friend from my own home was come to seek to be cured by him. The Doctor said he was ready to see him at once, and he added:

"I feel sure that you have the courage and coolness to assist at operations. Will you be present?"

I said I would, and I fetched in the road-mender. The Doctor examined him, and the man did not wince, and I saw the back of an eye for the first time. The Doctor said the operation was a serious one, but he had hope of its success; the road-mender must rest till next morning, and he would then see him again, at eleven punctually.

Of course we were there to the minute; a young Doctor was there too as assistant. I need not tell you about the preparations, the man was very patient and docile, and Bonifacia knelt on the floor in a corner of the room, praying. I took instructions as to how I was to hand this thing and that thing. The patient said it was quite unnecessary to bind him to a chair, he would sit quite still without, but he was quite content to let himself be tied all the same.

The Doctor was quite calm, but I could see by the assistant's face that it was a bad business. The Doctor made a little cut, then I instantly handed him another instrument, and he called out: "I have the splinter!" The man wanted to jump up, he cried out:

"I can see!" But we held him down, he had to shut his eye, and I helped to tie the bandage over them. The Doctor's face beamed with pleasure; I had to take Bonifacia out of the room, she cried so loud; when I came back into the room the Doctor gave me the tiny splinter of stone in a piece of paper, and said:

"Keep that in remembrance of the first time you assisted at an operation. I hope you will continue to do so; you have a steady and sure hand."

It was all I could do not to shout for joy —what! I might help in curing the suffering —I?

Bonifacia begged me to give her the splinter; Ronymus must have it set in gold and fastened to a ring; so I gave her the splinter, for I was sure the Doctor would think it right.

In the house and all through the village it was one great rejoicing among the sufferers over the wonderful cure of the road-mender; Bonifacia was ready to tell it to anyone who wanted to hear. They stayed with us three days; the Doctor taught me how to put on and take off bandages, and when he said I did it well—if God himself had come down from heaven and praised me, I could not have been happier.

Bonifacia and her husband must have told

the Doctor, who I was and where I came from, for he said to me:

"I could not help fancying that you must be descended from a respectable house and honest parents."

O, merciful God! what more could the world give me?

The parting with Bonifacia and her husband touched me nearly, still it did me good too. There is nothing better in the world than the last sight of folks to whom you have been able to do kindness; they go away carrying with them good recollections of you. And I had to go too before long.

After the cure of the road-mender I was present at every operation and held everything ready. One day a pupil of the Doctor's came from Zürich, and helped in operations and performed some himself too, to the satisfaction of his master who had a great love for him. The Doctor said to him once in my presence:

"My dear colleague, Brigitta is an admirable assistant; her readiness of hand may be depended on to a hair.—You should take her into your institution."

The Professor from Zürich asked me if I would go with him, and I accepted; but not till the autumn when our season would be over. And so in the autumn I left Heyden, and went to the Professor at Zürich.

———

CHAPTER XX.

THE way in which the Professor introduced me to his wife and the servants showed what he thought of me. He entrusted everything to me, and I never betrayed his confidence till that once—

It was a particular pleasure to me that the house dog—of whom I shall have much to say, his name was Rack—took to me greatly from the very first minute.

I soon saw that such an establishment as this was a very different thing from an inn. At first I felt as if I had been enchanted in some subterranean castle such as we read of in fairy tales. There were so many folks, and all as if they were under some spell, they could not do the smallest thing for themselves; there were ever so many dark rooms, and you felt as if all the world was ill. But I soon found my-

self at home there, and the blind folks were
very fond of me.

When I looked out of window in the morning with the lake lying before me, and the
Alps standing so high and all round me, while
that tiny sphere, the eye, can take them all
in—mountains and valleys, that are so vastly
larger than itself—then I first properly understood how the patients could vow that they
would never complain of anything again if
only they could recover their eyesight.

Every morning of my life I thanked God
that I had all my limbs sound and healthy,
and my own good eyes so that I could help
others.

I may say that I never was out of patience
or even cross, except that one time of which I
must tell you presently. The patients felt too
how I behaved to them—not quite the same to
all but to each according to his mind and
understanding, and many a one did me more
benefit than I did them. Aye, folks of all
classes and ranks and ages came into our

house; in such an establishment, under operations and afterwards during the cure, the real nature of a man shows itself, you cannot make believe or deceive yourself or others. As to religions I must say at once that there is no difference in the way in which the sick call upon God; the character and temper of each one, that is the chief thing. There are men whom it is a pleasure to serve, and to make up for that there are others who are dreadful, always cross and always venomous. The only thing is never to show any annoyance and at last you cease to feel any.

In the course of nearly seven years I had to nurse Catholics and Protestants and Jews and even Infidels—royal personages, who slept under silk coverlids, and had hands as delicate as the inside skin of an egg, and then again poor wild creatures, who in all their lives had never known what a bed was. From a man's thankfulness as he shows it and remembers it after he is cured, you first really know what he is, and I must say, in that the Jews are parti-

10*

cularly good; the professor too always said that
a Jew did not easily forget the good that had
been done him. Certainly the Jews are very
complaining, and are always very sorry for
themselves, but as I have said they are particularly grateful.

Once we had three priests together in the
house at the same time, a Catholic, a Lutheran,
and a Jew. Our Lord must have heard how
they all prayed to him differently. The two
Christian priests were cured, but not the Jew.
When at last we were obliged to tell him, he
said:

"Praised be the Lord, who allowed me to
see for so many years; I know the scriptures
all by heart and can read them without eyes."
And he thanked us warmly for all the patience
and affection we had shown him. To the Professor he said: You thought to do your
best, but God thought it was good for me
that it should be otherwise; he knows wherefore."

We had a princess too in the house, from

Thuringia I think, a very fine, tall woman; she never uttered a sound of complaint, neither during the operation nor afterwards, and only one eye was saved. When I did anything for her she would stroke my cheek or my hand with her soft hand and say a word or two, little wise and kind things I could never tell you. Not a thought of pride had she. There was a shepherd in the house who was stone-blind, he lost his way once in the passage and came into the Princess's room, she led him by the hand to his own. The old man said to the Professor: "You must write down for me in my hymn-book that a princess led me by the hand and called me her good friend."

Over the princess lived an old peasant woman, who used to tell us how one day she let her little grand-child fall, she picked it up again, and the child screamed fearfully till her daughter came in, and the grandmother had turned it upside down on her arm. People laughed at the idea of such an old woman wanting to be cured.

I am no more than a peasant myself—but
I must say when I compare educated people
with many peasant-folks it often seemed to me
that these were no more than half men; they
were so uncouth, so avaricious and suspicious,
and hardly knew how to do anything for themselves.

But we had one good soul in the establishment who guided me rightly in everything.
When I begin to talk about that wise, good
woman—the wife of a doctor from the Palatinate
—I never know when to stop. She had only a
glimmer of eyesight, but she was so handy that
she needed hardly any help. I only had to
read to her as often as I had time, and it was
as good as school to me; she explained everything to me, she understood everything, and in
her room and in her mind everything was in
perfect order. Properly speaking she was no
longer a patient, and she wanted to leave the
house and make way for some one else; but
the professor and his wife would not let her go,
she was as helpful as if she had been physician

and priest and housekeeper all in one. Aye—
she was a real blessing to the house. Those
who had lost all hope and courage turned to
her, sheltering under her, as you may see with
a brood-hen; and her voice—well, it is not right
when I say it was like a brood-hen's, and yet
there was something like that in it—I mean
something comforting and warm and protect-
ing, a motherly attraction.

Just as each patient needs his particular
medicine, so each needs his particular form of
comfort. She listened patiently to each one's
complaining, and that in itself did them good,
and a few encouraging words raised their spirits.
Often it is not the· pain that torments the
suffering, the tediousness hurts them much
more.

There were young girls there who did not
know a bit what to do with themselves, and
tried all kinds of things; she taught them different kinds of handiwork, and to practise
and prepare in case of the worst, so that
they might still be of some use to

themselves and others, and not helpless burthens.

It is hard to be blind, no doubt, but the fear of becoming blind is worse still. That good lady strengthened many a one to endure the inevitable. "Never forget my child," she would often say, "that from patience springs love, as we are told in the gospel. The blind must ask many questions because they cannot see, and never let yourself be out of patience with them, for you do not know what that eternal darkness is—what it is never to lift your foot, but always to shuffle and slip about, feeling with your hands and feet; not to see the morsel you are putting into your mouth, not a flower, not a gleam, not a human countenance; have patience and it will grow into love in yourself and in others."

CHAPTER XXI.

I MUST tell you about some of the others—not about all, that would be too long, but I must recall a few more before the last who came—

We had a lady in the house, a Baroness of Haueisen too; she was a cousin of the Baron's; but I never told her that I had known him—she could not help his being her cousin; and she was very different, as gentle as an angel. Three times I had to read her a letter from her cousin in Italy. I did not do this gladly, but in my place what I liked had nothing to do with it. The Captain's letter was as methodical and affectionate as if it had been written by a good honest man. He was taking life easily, and never thought of how things were going on with those whom he had plundered.

The Baroness wanted to dictate to me an

answer to his letter, but I escaped that; I could not write kind and loving words to that man. The Baroness Haueisen was a noble and thoroughly good-hearted lady; all of one family even are not alike. She said to me once:

"I must acknowledge it as God's guidance that I have suffered so much; it was not till then that I learned how much love and kind helpfulness there are in the world." She went away cured and thanked us in most touching terms.

Aye—nothing more beautiful and nothing better ever flows from the human heart than at the moment when a patient who is cured takes his leave. Many a one could not speak at all but has written to me from home. Still everything was not always smooth and well at the establishment; many patients, especially those who had hurt themselves by drink, were quite unmanageable, and once one went mad on the third day. He was an emigration-agent, who had shipped off many poor souls to countries where they soon died. He must have been in

the habit of calling them gulls and boobies—
for he kept on shouting the words, till they got
him into a strait-waistcoat.

I had not thought of the Captain at all for
a long time, but now, when this man went mad
in remorse for his past misdeeds, I could not
help thinking of the Captain. Would he end so
likewise?

But once more I had to divert my thoughts
from this subject.

Of course we had to have most patience
with children. Once a father and mother
brought us a child saying it was so naughty
that it never would be quiet till it was flogged.
I spoke to the child, and it promised me that
it would be quite quiet during the operation
and more particularly after it, and it kept its
word and I was quite happy everything went so
well. This child had a character as strong as a
man's and at the same time as submissive and
as conscientious; she did not venture to speak
or stir and kept as still as if she had been dumb
and motionless. She grew up a fine girl, and is

now employed in the telegraph-office at the Station at Zürich.

I must still tell you about Seridja and the professor of astronomy—it belongs to the next event that happened to me, and by whose agency?—by the Captain's.

.

CHAPTER XXII.

ONE day the Professor said to me that I must go away from the institute for a short time, for that the English lady from India, whom I had already seen at Heyden had come with her child—the child's eyes had been badly operated on, and were now worse than ever. The operation would not be performed in the house but at the hotel Bauer down by the lake, and so they would have to stay there while she recovered from the effects.

I was very unwilling to go out of the house, I could not bear to think that I should ever quit it, but my friend the doctor's wife was right; I was but a soldier who was placed at his post, and I should presently be released from it. So I moved down to the hotel, and who should be standing under the inn-gate with a large green apron on but Ronymus?

He gave me a glance of recognition, otherwise he gave no sign that he knew me.

The English lady lived high up in the hotel and I was at once announced. Ronymus pushed aside another hostler, took my box on his shoulder, carried it to the lift in which folks go up and down, and said:

"Step in here."

I obeyed him, he stepped in too, the machine made a gurgling noise and up it went; in the little room in which we went up there was a light burning as if it were night; I thought I was bewitched.

"Did you know me at once?" asked Ronymus, and he passed his hand across his eyes as he spoke:

"Yes."

"But we will not let other folks see that we know each other. Oh! merciful God! oh, good God! Why is it—"

But he said no more, we were soon up at the third floor; the machine stood still, Ronymus took my box on his shoulder again, and carried it into my room. He wiped the sweat off his face with a handkerchief; but he went on wiping and did not cease—he dried something else away, and breathed hard.

"I often carry seven times as much quite easily," he said at length. "Why at your place I have shouldered a sack of oats, and carried it to the top loft like a feather. Say—did you know that I was here?"

"No."

"But I knew that you were here; I wrote to tell my parents. I have known it long, but I did not want to cause you any inconvenience. Could I say I was servant in your father's house? I was afraid I might betray myself— betray you—"

The good fellow could say no more, and it struck through all my limbs like a flash of lightning: "Ronymus is in love with you!" Nay, the faithful soul should not be made unhappy by me. I think that some of my pride as a descendant of peasant proprietors clung about me yet, and I was accustomed too to something superior—I said: .

"I am very happy at the establishment, and I shall stay there all my life."

"Aye—aye—" said he. "And I must tell you too that I know all that you did for my father and mother. I will not let any understrapper clean your shoes—I will clean them everyday myself; I would lie down for you to walk over. Don't look so astonished. Be thankful you have a man near you, who — Hush! here is some one coming.— Have you any farther commands?" he added hastily in quite another voice—the rogue.

Our Professor came in and Ronymus went away; but the professor must have noticed something, for he said:

"Gitta, you look quite concerned. Do you find it so hard to leave the establishment? Never mind, you will soon be comfortable here, and you will have much more time at your disposal. I should not like to have you for

my assistant to-day; let me feel your pulse—
yes, you are feverish."

I had a touch of fever no doubt; not on
account of Ronymus, that matter I could soon
set right without fail, but the old life seemed to
come over me and down upon me, and I had
almost forgotten where I had come from, and
what had formerly happened.

But it is a fine thing to be young, and even
better to have a noble duty to fulfil. I was a
soldier placed at my post—that came back into
my mind, and it was my duty to be vigilant
and not to trouble myself about anything
beyond.

The professor now explained to me that I
should have a particularly difficult task to keep
the little red-haired girl quiet; she was a perfect
little devil, to whom we might give chloroform
indeed, but whom it was impossible to cure in
this excited state. "But you know what Seridja
was at Heyden."

He then took me to the child, and
said :

"Here, Seridja, I have brought a kind friend to see you."

As soon as I went near the child, she screamed out as if she had been stuck on a spit, and when I stooped down she tried to clutch my hair, and struck me in the face with both fists.

"Surely, my child, you did not mean to hit me?" said I. "I dare say you have some bad pain that makes you so naughty and cross? You wanted to hit your pain away."

As I spoke, she shrieked out:

"Go away, go away, I don't want you.— No, stay there, stay a little; what is your name?"

"Gitta."

"Gitta—that is funny, Gitta, Gitta—Come, give me your hand—I will not hurt you; yes, it is the pain that is so naughty and cross." I gave her my hand and she stroked it.

Her mother and the Professor looked at each other, and their thoughts were the same as mine: The child is conquered, I have her under my hand.

———

CHAPTER XXIII.

THE Professor went away, and in the ante-
room he said it was very clever of me to have
spoken so to the child, but it was not clever in
the least, it was what I really meant, and if it
had not been so it would not have been of the
least use. The child was not tame at once
from that first day forth, but whenever I said I
should go away she would beg me to forgive
her, and give me everything she had. I may
say it was impossible to be more patient than
I was with Seridja, and I helped her mother
who could no longer do anything with her own
child. Good God! here was a vigorous high-
spirited creature, that would have been fain to
skip and jump, and there she must lie—she
could not play with anything—had never seen
anything of the world around her—had nothing
to remember and could not know whether she

was in Rome or Constantinople or Zurich. In
the thirteen years of her life she had been in
all sorts of countries, knew a number of lan-
guages—knew the name for a dog in a dozen
tongues and did not know what a dog looked
like.—It was a bitter lot.

Her mother now got better, she could leave
her child for hours or even half the day and
get fresh air; she had been quite worn out.
When the Professor came again I said that he
must give the child our good dog Rack. He
asked me whether she had expressed any wish
to have a dog; I told him it was only my own
idea, for that she must have some living thing
to play with. The Professor brought Rack.
The good beast blinked its kindly honest eyes
at me as much as to say: 'I know too that the
poor child is blind, and we two will let her
tease us or caress us just as may be.' Seridja
was quite delighted with Rack. I had to tell
her what the dog looked like, he was a fine
black setter with long ears and a white muzzle,
white marks and white feet. The little girl

would talk for hours to Rack, and this was a
great relief to her mother. I had to sleep with
Seridja and tell her stories till she fell asleep.
I told her all the stories I knew, and stories
out of my life too; when I told her about our
lost geese and how they came back and gobbled
and cackled and croaked, she imitated the
geese as I did, and I had to perform that again
and again.

I never told her anything of our life when
we were rich but of my having broken stones
on the road, and the child called out: "Mother,
Gitta must have gone through harder trials
than the princess in the fairy-tale, she kept
geese and gathered berries in the wood, but she
never broke stones.   Gitta, you will be much
more than a Queen." ·

We laughed at her, and sharp as she was
and clever in her questions, she wanted to
know whether stones were easier to break, in
rain or in sunshine—she wanted to know everything.

I told her too how the road-mender had

had a splinter of stone fly in his eye—but, oh
woe! the child shrieked like one possessed; she
fancied she had a splinter in her own eye,
and cried·like mad: "Take it out, take it
out."

All was spoilt now for some days. Her
mother scolded me for having told the child
such a thing and I reproached myself too; but
I had nothing more to tell her, and she would
not be read to out of books; indeed I had
learnt many stories by heart.

Something else came into my mind again;
I knew many songs of the oak-barkers and of
Bonifacia's, so I sang them to Seridja and she
learnt all the songs very quickly; she had a
pretty voice, and we sang together, it went as if
they were made on purpose.

It is particularly good for a convalescent to
be cheerful. The Professor had every confidence
in the success of the operation, only the child
must be quiet and patient during her recovery,
else it would be all in vain—nay, worse than
before.

I was often very angry with her mother; a lady of her quality should on no account have allowed her child to grow so refractory and unmanageable; the little girl was a perfect tyrant; from the first thing in the morning till the last thing at night some one must incessantly be telling her stories or doing something to amuse her. I often was at my wit's end what to do next.

Then a good idea occurred to me. I begged the child to teach me English; this pleased her greatly. Each day I was to learn so many words and phrases, and she was quite delighted to play schoolmistress. I learnt to speak English fluently; now, to be sure, I have forgotten it again.

CHAPTER XXIV.

AND how was Ronymus getting on?

Very well; he has a straightforward considerate way with him, he takes much after his father. He told me that he had saved something already and that he hoped to do better yet. His life as a soldier had made quite a new man of him; he told me that the Swiss were very glad to get Germans as waiters, particularly those who had served as soldiers. He never teased me with love-making, not with a single word, and I even thought it had been my fancy and that I troubled myself unnecessarily. He was respectful to me, only he could never make up his mind to my being a servant —I, the Princess of Schlchenhof—and a sick-nurse too.

Before the English lady we made no secret of having known each other ever since we were

children, and Ronymus must have told her at
some time or other that I was of good family.
As often as opportunity offered the English
lady liked to talk with Ronymus, he is so
straightforward and at the same time full of
fun; he was very happy to see his little fortune
increasing day by day—he had already bought
two fields and a pasture at home. But Ronymus was quite different from me; he liked to
think of the past and rejoiced in seeing that
things had improved, I on the contrary could
not bear to remember the past.

Ronymus is just the same to this day, he
recalls his former poverty at every opportunity, and is always thankful for all the
present time gives him, whatever it may be.

One day, when I complained to Ronymus
that the English lady spoiled everything I did
to improve the child, he said:

"How can you be vexed with that lady?
Why she is just a simpleton, as empty as bean-
straw?"

I saw it when he said it—you may be dull-

witted in the finest clothes and with the greatest
wealth; everything was clearer to me after that
and I was no longer vexed with the lady; she
was simply stupid and had no insight. As I
have said Ronymus spared me all love-making,
only once he said:

"What do you think now a pair of good
eyes may be worth?"

"Oh, you flatterer!"

"Flatterer! how a flatterer? I don't mean
your eyes but my own. The patients here
could tell you what the value of good eyes is;
but it is as well that they cannot buy them, for
if they could we should have to go about blind.
And when good. eyes first look kindly—Hey!
there's the bell again."

"Aye—take yourself off." And Ronymus
went.

One day I had been into the town on some
business and on my return to the hotel I went
up in the lift; I was standing, on the seat were

a lady with veil on and a man who also
wore a veil; I could hardly see them in
the dimly lighted room, but I heard the lady
say:

"If you will be ill, why be thoroughly ill—
go into a hospital, but I am not going to turn
sick nurse."

The man sighed, but said nothing.

They both got out at the first floor. I went
on higher, but I could not get rid of the im-
pression, I felt as if I had heard the lady's
voice before. Could they have been the Captain and his wife? But I scolded myself for
my silly notions. The next day I asked Ronymus to enquire at the bureau of the hotel,
whether the Captain and his wife had not been
there.

"There is no need for asking; one of our
omnibus drivers was his jockey, and he got him
into trouble; he knew him again directly. Aye
—he it was, but they are gone away again.
He came to consult your professor; he has

grown older and she too, but he dyes his beard and she paints her cheeks. It was talked of all over the house how those two quarrelled. She went to the table d'hôte alone, smartly dressed, and when his food was brought to him she would sit in the balcony; she did not choose to see how he eat. I carried down their trunks. He can still see a little and he held up his eyelids with his fingers and looked at me as much as to say: 'I have seen you before, only I don't know where I saw you.—But I know where I should like to see him, the wretch —who kills trees and kills men, the villain! If ever I go to heaven I will ask one thing only of God Almighty, and that is for two hours' leave one day, that I may go down into hell and give the Captain a thrashing; he shall learn then what I can do; it will be my greatest bliss."

"You are very wicked. I will never think of the Captain again. If we have evil thoughts of any man that is the way we lose our own souls."

"Aye, aye, maybe you're right — and there is no need for it; the man is punished enough — he has a bad wife — that is quite enough."

———————

CHAPTER XXV.

I HAD plenty now to do and to think about, there was no time for any other thoughts even; presence of mind and of body both were indispensable. We gave Seridja chloroform, and the operation was performed with ease and in the regular course. When she woke up again I implored her neither to speak nor move, and she said nothing but 'Rack.'

The dog understood; he went up to the bed, laid his head on the edge of the mattrass, and the child laid her hand on his head, and so the two remained for hours silent and motionless. I had now only to soothe the mother, who was quite beside herself with terror and wanted to make her child speak.

It is a good thing to know when a body is somewhat daft; then one can have patience; otherwise one really could not.

It is always best when the first bandage can be left on as long as possible; I told Seridja this, and I saw how she set her teeth and silently clutched the dog, but they both remained silent and motionless. I sat with her in the darkened room; outside it was day—we saw nothing of it; outside were noise and bustle —I could hear nothing but the child's breathing and the dog's, who sighed deeply now and then.

All went well; when the little girl was allowed to speak for the first time, she said :

"I thought I was breaking stones with you, and bright sparks of fire flew out, and they sang to me so sweetly and softly — but not songs, only pretty tinkling sounds."

The child was like a different creature, and she helped me soothe her mother who was always wanting to kiss and clasp her in her arms. She cried for joy and I was in the greatest terror lest she should make Seridja cry too, but she mastered herself bravely. We gradually accustomed the child to the light, and my own eyes filled with tears when she said: "I see you, mother, and I see you, Gitta, and I see you, Rack."

The day came when we could venture for the first time to go on the Lake. It was a grey cloudy day with no sun in the sky, Seridja kissed my hand and said:

"See how delighted Rack is, I am sure if he could, he would say how glad he is that I can see. Oh! the trees and the water and the men and the houses and the boats—"

Of course I kept Seridja's spirits down as much as possible, and she was still for a time; but presently she called out again:

"Oh! how large and wide it all is—how wide the world is, and how high the sky is—but I feel as if I could hug it all!

Every one who met us looked at us as if they knew that Seridja had been blind; they stood still to gaze at the child. Indeed a prettier creature can never have been seen; she had auburn curling hair, and her whole face was like the most beautiful picture, and above all her eyes! they were of the loveliest violet-blue and shone so! her whole face seemed to beam as if it shone by a light of its own.

Now, for the first time could Seridja really ask questions; the first time we went out on the high road she pointed to the little broken stones, picked one up and wanted to know what shape they must be broken into — she could not find any square ones—and which were the best kinds of stone. Her questions quite bewildered me.

I thought I ought now to go home again, but the Professor said that the mother might spoil everything even yet, so I must remain and keep strict watch. We sailed several times all round the Lake I had for so many years seen from above; once too we went up the Rigi and spent the night there. There were a number of folks who were delighted with the sunrise, naturally Seridja above all. For my own part I must say, it was fine, but just nothing very particular.

Well—I went back to the Professor's establishment with Rack. The dog loudly expressed his joy at being at home again; I went
silently and slowly up the hill.

Aye—and with regard to Rack both Seridja
and her mother were very cruel and ungrateful
to me. Seridja wished to keep the dog, and I
was too hasty—I ought to have let the Professor decide and speak first; however, I said
the dog was a benefactor to all the patients,
and that one single one ought not to keep him.
The Professor agreed with me; but Seridja's
fine eyes could look very wicked—very spiteful
and hard. She had never learned before that
anyone could refuse her anything and her voice
was quite altered when, as I took leave, she
said:

"You can go, and the dog with you—Go, be
off with you—"

Seridja and her mother left the hotel soon
after, and lived quietly in a country villa near
the Lake. They were waiting for Seridja's
father who was to arrive from India, but they

12*

waited in vain for a long time, and the re-
mittances of money failed too.

It was Ronymus now who found money for
mother and daughter, and helped them in every
way—of course he got some advantage out of
this. One day he came to me, and said:
"Now I am coming to the point.—The English lady has given me a necklace to pledge
for her; I went off and asked what it might be
worth, and it is worth a great deal, there is not
another like it in all Switzerland; but the pawn-
broker will only lend one third of the value of
the pledged property. It strikes me you might
do as much as that, and if the necklace were
never redeemed you would have three times
the money, and good interest in any case."

I must confess I was greatly pleased with
Ronymus, he had more in him than I thought;
but I would have nothing to do with lending
and borrowing, I had had enough to suffer from
that. Indeed I must confess too that I was
still smarting from the ingratitude shown me
by Seridja and her mother. They no longer

knew me—they no longer needed me. I was least vexed with the mother, she was a silly woman, and I have come to know other people of small wits who were thankless; but Seridja —I had to get over it, but it pained me.

The father arrived from India, and he went away with his wife and daughter—they never came to take leave of me.

Ronymus came and informed me what good luck he had had; the English gentleman had paid him everything in hard cash, and had given him a good bit of money into the bargain.

"Properly speaking," said he, and he gave me a strange look; "properly speaking I ought to give you half of it since I owe it to you that I came to know the English lady so well. But I think we may leave the two halves together, and have the money between us."

I understood full well what he meant but I said nothing about it.

I made some complaint about ingratitude

to the doctor's widow; she took all I had
to say quite patiently, and then she said:

"You are always forgetting that there are
wicked men in the world; do not let this mis-
lead you into being hard-hearted towards
others. How can they help it, that they should
suffer for it? And if we consider the matter
rightly we need no reward nor thanks. We do
good to our neighbour because it is right, and
there is reward enough in the happiness of doing good. There are men whom no suffering
nor misery can improve, and yet the doctrine of
scripture is that blessedness proceeds from
suffering."

She must have seen in me that I was thinking: "How comes it that this woman can talk
about the world in this way, as if she could have
nothing to do with it? and yet she goes with
the world, in an honest way."

She must have seen this, for she said:

"Gitta, I am soon going to leave, and I do
not know whether I shall ever see you again in
this world. I do not wish for death, but I

await it patiently. Still I must tell you my little history—it may be of use to you too."

The doctor's widow told me her story. I feel as if I could hear her speaking now, and could repeat it after her, word for word.

———

CHAPTER XXVI.

"I DO not know whether you knew it before but I will tell you now—I was a Jewess and I became a Christian. I was baptised at the same time as my husband, soon after our marriage. My husband was an unbeliever; all forms of creed were the same to him. So long as the Jews had not the same rights as Christians he would never become a Christian, for he thought it infamous to gain any temporal advantages by a change of religion. But the new laws effaced all civic differences between the adherents of the two religions, and then we had ourselves baptised in a Protestant church. My husband, however, remained an unbeliever; I for my part have a fervent love for Jesus Christ, who, by his living and his teaching, stands above every other.

Certainly what some priests make of Him

is barely recognisable; and He would drive many of those who confess His name out of His temple if he were to see how they treat all who do not follow him, and especially the Jews. If the apostles themselves were alive now they would be called 'converted Jews' with utter contempt, for men of Christian parentage use the word with a certain tone of scorn.

My husband was a physician in good practice, full of zeal for his calling and always one of the first and foremost when there was anything to be done for the good of the people or of the country. Then came the revolution of 1848, and, the year after, the provisional government in our country. My husband was called on to serve in it; it was overthrown, my husband was carried to prison and threatened with death under martial-law.* In the state in which I was I suffered more than I can tell you. My child was born dead, and as my life was in danger, my husband was allowed to visit

* The country being proclaimed for the time in a state of siege.

me as I lay in bed. Two soldiers with muskets and side arms came with him into my room; I will not tell you what we suffered, but we stood it firmly. We saw each other for the last time. I got well again, so far as health goes; my husband died in prison, but I did not know it till some weeks after when I was recovering from an attack of fever.

My husband was buried in the Protestant cemetery attached to the citadel; I had to go into southern Switzerland for the sake of my delicate chest.

I could go on telling you about it all day; every one seemed to set to work to embitter my soul, but without success; they no more succeeded in that, than in breaking and sub-duing the spirit of my forefathers by two cen-turies of torture and repression. But I will only tell you one thing. I lived in a boarding-house in which almost everyone was German. It was a pleasant and social life till a priest from—but I will not name the place or it might hurt the feelings of the other inhabitants—a priest, in short, came who also was an invalid.

It was easy to see that I was a Jewess—my hair was as black as coal—and now there began endless whisperings and mutterings about which I did not trouble myself greatly.

The priest felt strong enough to exercise his office, and he preached in the bitterest terms against the Jews, appealing to texts in the Bible. All turned to look at me, and they could plainly see by my face that I disagreed with this application of the text. The priest had availed himself for the occasion of an angry word of the Apostle's uttered in the midst of the struggle for the establishment of the new doctrine. He did not understand the sublime grandeur of Jesus Christ, nor the glorious message of salvation that says all mankind are the children of God.

· I went into the sitting-room — all shrunk from me; I saw that I was in disgrace and under a ban; I left that house and went into another.

I could easily have said that I had been baptised, but I was ashamed that human souls could bear the Redeemer's name and yet behave thus.

A noble gentleman of Pomerania—he was a Captain in the army too—was the only one who took my part. He had previously known no one of Hebrew origin or of the Jewish faith, but he held it a duty to protect those who were persecuted by the uncharitable and cruel. As I saw his honourable and truly humane character I told him I was a Christian. He was an earnest and faithful Christian, but from that day he quarrelled with the dogmas of the creed.

I may venture to say that it was I who succeeded in keeping him steadfast to a pure belief in God.

I must confess, however, that rage and hatred boiled within me, but I wrestled with these evil spirits till I could say to myself: 'No, the wicked shall not so far trouble me as to poison my heart. No, I will do all the good

I can to those who falsely call themselves
Christians and followers of the religion of love.
One thing certainly I cannot do, I cannot love
my enemies, and I know no one who can; nay,
I believe the saying was never meant in that
sense, only, as it is written afterwards: I can
and I must do good to those who have injured me.

But go now, Gitta—merely telling it has
stirred my soul—"

So spoke the doctor's widow. She often sat
with a fixed gaze as if she were addressing
some invisible person, and as I looked at her,
her face was lighted up by a gleam of tender
melancholy and the sublime victory over the
world. I did not stir from the spot, and I
could have embraced the knees of the much-
enduring lady, but she never could bear anything of that sort. I asked her what had become of the Pomeranian Captain, and she said
he had died soon after; she had nursed him till
his latest breath.

I was going away, but she said:

"No, stay a little, it is best now when some one is with me." And we sat together in silence for a long time; I remained with her till she fell asleep.

A few days later I accompanied her to the railway, the professor and his wife were there too.

I met Ronymus, and he said to me:

"I have money enough now, I shall not go on with my work here any longer. Schmaje is looking out for a convenient inn for us, with some fields and pasture and a bit of forest as well; then we shall have everything."

"Who are 'we?'"

Ronymus looked down at the ground, and drew a deep breath; then he said:

"Hah! my father and I. It is a pity my mother could not live to see it—"

He paused, seeing what a blow it was to me to learn it so; then he went on:

"She died easily, and in her very last hour she thought of you, but I cannot tell you all that now."

I went home to the establishment, the way
up the hill was harder than it had ever been;
may be I had a forecast in my mind of what
was coming upon me. And Bonifacia was
dead! that faithful soul. How was the road-
mender living, and how did things look, out
there in the little cottage? As I thought this
I seemed to see the leaves falling from the
trees, and that autumn day when I first met
the Captain rose up in my memory. Why does
this always recur to my mind?

This winter again we had the house full,
and I sadly missed the good doctor's wife.
Often and often I felt as if I must go to her
and gain counsel from her; I could no longer
rely on myself alone. But at last I said to
myself: 'Come; this must not be. You who
have to help and sustain so many others must
not need help yourself.'

I took up my duties again just as if I were
beginning for the first time; it was a real
pleasure to me, and I found it quite easy to go
upstairs and down from one to another, do-

ing something for each. In the room that had been the doctor's widow's there now lived an elegant, but very delicate lady, who had literally gone blind with crying, after her husband's death. Our Professor thought it would be difficult to do anything for her, and although she was so feeble, he allowed her to play the pianoforte almost the whole day. Her husband had been a famous musician, she was his pupil, and had run away with him; he died early and now she played all sorts of pieces to his memory.

We had too a famous Professor of astronomy, who had spoilt his sight in his pursuits. He was under my special care, and our Professor said he would be cured; he was a very loveable, patient, old gentleman, and received visits from all parts—distinguished and elegant men and women — and they all thanked me for my good care of him.

O merciful God! there are so many good folks in the world, and why should' one, such a thorough scoundrel, have come to my father's farm and have ruined us?

The astronomer left us cured. We are always glad when the patients leave us cured, but the parting from such a good superior man is a great grief.

The astronomer's room was newly furnished and a second room was added to it; it was said we were soon to receive a very distinguished patient, of great pretensions, and I was told off to his particular service.

Why was I so uneasy and anxious? What had troubled me with a painful forboding actually came to pass—the Captain arrived.

CHAPTER XXVII.   ˙

IT was midday when a carriage drove up.
I looked out of the window—a tall and stately
man was helped out. I felt as if I must fall
out of window—I felt as if I must drop backwards—Merciful God! There was the Captain.
—And must I nurse him and wait upon him?
On *him?*—No, that I would not—I would not
stop in the house—I would not stay under the
same roof with that man.

He was led upstairs, I heard his step in the
next room, then his voice — I had not been
mistaken, it was he. Our Professor opened
the door between the rooms, and said to
me :

"Come in here."

I do not know how I found the strength
to go into the other room. There sat the Captain in an arm-chair ; his eyes were bandaged

and his hands were clasped in front of him. The professor said:

"Here is your new charge. I know you are patient—mind you are particularly so with this gentleman."

I could not even bring out 'Yes'—my throat felt as if I were being strangled. The Captain asked:

"What is your name?"

I could not utter my own name, and the Professor said:

"She is called Gitta. Why do you look so blank? You are usually—"

The Captain interrupted him by asking:

"Is she old or young?"

"Young."

"Where is she?"

I could not stir from the spot where I stood, and the Professor said to me:

"Why are you so childish all of a sudden?"

Childish, he said—and I felt as if I must cry out and say: 'I am the child of the man who was brought to ruin and harried to death

13*

by this man.' But I did not utter a word, and the Captain said:

"Step nearer, come here."

He spoke commandingly, pulled off his glove and put out his hand and the Professor led me up to him, taking me by the arm. I had to give my hand to that thief—that murderer! He said:

"Why do you tremble? You have nothing to fear from me—I am a poor, forsaken blind man." And he broke into sobs that came from his heart. I felt no pity for him; I clenched my fists, I could have hit him in the breast with both hands, and have cried out: 'You robbed my father, you murderer, my father!'

Our Professor counselled him to be strong and a man, telling him he must not cry, for that it would postpone the operation—which must be a difficult one even without that aggravation—for days, perhaps for weeks.

The new assistant now came in; he had only been with us for a short time and had been an army-surgeon in Germany. The two

Doctors sent me away and proceeded once more to make an examination. I stood outside in the ante-room, and again the feeling came over me that I would not stop in the house an hour longer — that I could not. I would tell the Professor why I must leave, and he should not cure the villainous wretch—he should never see a tree again, nor a flower, nor a human face; he should remain blind, and 'go down quick into the pit'—

The Professor came out of the room, and said to me:

"Your new patient is the very reverse of the astronomer, who was pure good-heartedness; this one is full of spite and venom against the whole world because suffering has come upon him. Still child, we must not stop to consider whether he is good or evil; all we know is that he is suffering and we must help him as far as we are able. If your new patient is ill-tempered he must be treated with all the more good temper; I have every confidence in your doing this."

He went down stairs with his assistant, and I could hear the assistant say:

"Do not mention my name to this man; I know him of old, I was in his regiment."

"Indeed—then you must tell me about him. He has evidently been a very violent man, that I have seen myself. I ought not properly to have taken him into the house, and yet I have done so." Then he named some disease, in Latin.

The sound of their steps died away; I stood on the landing of the staircase, and had to cling to the balustrade—I was so dizzy. Now again came into my mind what the Doctor's wife had said to me: 'We cannot force ourselves to love our enemy, but we can force ourselves to help him and to do good to him.' This I must do—I can and I will.

CHAPTER XXVIII.

I WENT into the room; the Captain was standing at the window. He turned round and said:

"Is that you, Schaller?"

My heart quaked within me. Then Schaller was to come too? He would know me again. I said that it was I, and he answered roughly:

"Go. No—stay. Tell me what is to be seen out of the window here?"

I told him that in front of this window there was a tall fir-tree and not much could be seen, but that from the other window you looked over the Lake and the Alps.

"You have a singular voice," said he. "Are you Swiss?" But he did not wait for an answer, and asked again:

"Where is the music that we can hear now?"

"On a steamer on the Lake. The wind often brings the sound up here."

"Aye, indeed—the world is merry; they sail on the Lake with music! Now go—stop; one thing more; never deceive me; I observe everything. Now go."

I went into the next room and was thankful to sit down. Now, should I not tell the Professor all the Captain had done to us at home? No—I could bear it best in silence—still, should I not tell Ronymus what I had to bear? No—not even Ronymus. I would do it all alone—

The Captain was whistling in his room; he whistled beautifully, whole long pieces of music.

The door opened and Rack came in.

"Is there not a dog with you?" called the Captain; he had wonderfully sharp ears. I said there was, and I told Rack to go to the gentleman, but for the first time he did not obey me

at once. I had to order him quite sternly. The
Captain felt the dog and said he was not of
pure breed but a cross of a sheep-dog and a
setter. Rack looked at me as if he understood
what he said; that dog was good-tempered to
everybody excepting the Captain. Who can
tell how a dog like that knows when a man is
not honest?

All the patients were generally pleased when
I told them about a clever trick of Rack's, and
I said to the Captain: "He is a very shrewd
dog; a watering-pot stands in a particular
corner, and when Rack is thirsty he takes the
handle of it in his mouth and carries the water-
can to someone to pour water into it; then he
laps it up with his long tongue, and carries it
back to its place again."

Rack shook his head all the while I was
speaking as if to say, 'you should not have told
the story to this man'—and he was right; for
the Captain said:

"I don't care for such stories."

Generally I could find all sorts of things

to tell the folks but now I could think of nothing more.

I had to lead the Captain by the hand, and tell him where everything stood in the large apartment—the tables, chairs and bed.

"Is there no looking-glass in the room?" said he. I said 'no,' and he laughed:

"To be sure, I could not see myself. Allow me—I want to feel what your face is like."

He passed his hand over my face, but I pushed him away with a blow of my fist which, as it would seem, was harder than it need have been, for he said:

"Well, well—it shall not occur again. Tell me, is it day or night?" I told him, the sun was just going down, and then he said again in his commanding tone:

"Go." He was accustomed to push men here and there, as if they were mere chattels. I stood by the window in the outer room, and looked out—Sky, earth and water were all pure glowing gold. I turned away, I know not why.

There, on the wall, hung the portrait of the great Berlin Doctor, and I could not help thinking: 'Oh! perhaps you too may once have had an enemy, at any rate you have cured bad men as well as good ones. You never had a wish but to do good—I cannot do what you can do, but what I can I will.' And as I thought this I fancied he smiled upon me.

Indeed it was very strange; for the next day the Professor told me that the great Doctor at Berlin had died at sunset the evening before. And at that very same hour I was thinking of him, and he must have felt in his dying moments to how many men he had restored the light of day.

CHAPTER XXIX.

THE next day the Captain was different, and so was I. When I woke in the morning and remembered who it was I had to attend upon I thought again that I could not and ought not; I could not be a true and faithful nurse to a man whom I could but curse from the bottom of my heart. Hitherto I had done my duty, now I should be unfaithful to my duty; I must tell this to the Professor. Then again I thought: 'What does it matter to you who the patient is? And is he not punished already; he can no longer live as he pleases, he must submit to others and have no will of his own; you cannot help feeling pity for him; besides, he is doubly wretched—blind and with a bad conscience.'

The Captain now called me, and asked me if it were yet day, and then he said he had certainly been cross and violent the day before, but I must not take it ill in him for he suffered keen pain, and troubles too which no instruments, however sharp, could remove.'

"I was blind even when I could see," he added.

Just as he said this the lady over head began to play the piano, and he cried out vehemently:

"That I will not stand—that must be put an end to."

I had to fetch the Professor, who explained to the Captain that he ought to try to take pleasure in the lady's beautiful playing instead of being angered by it; if this were not the case in two day's time he should have other rooms given him.

"And why should I move? why not that strumming woman?"

"I must beg you to speak to me somewhat more calmly," said the Professor. "You must learn to control yourself and submit; you aggravate your condition by your violence, and interfere with the treatment and cure."

The Captain then enquired quite calmly and gently, who it was that played the piano overhead, and the Professor told him of the lady who had gone blind with grieving for her lost husband and would soon consume her very vital powers.

"Is that true that you are telling me?"

The Professor answered quite sharply:

"Baron, I must desire that you will never use such language to me again. You are not a child, and I am not an inventor of romances."

The Captain saw that he was not a man to be trifled with. I must say I never saw the Professor so sharp to any other patient; and he must have known more about the Captain than I thought; at any rate he meant to master him.

The Captain spoke again quite gently: "I must beg you to forgive a much injured — I should say a much-enduring man. Then there really is such love in the world? I will believe it—I cannot but believe you."

When the Professor was gone and the lady was playing again, the Captain whistled to the music. Suddenly he called me and said I was to go up to the lady and ask if he might not go to her room and listen to her, nay he could play duets with her. I said that one patient might not send messages to another without the knowledge of the Professor, and then he shouted again:

"Damn it! are the patients here imprisoned convicts?"

I thought to myself: 'You ought to be a convict in fetters and chains;' all my hatred surged up again.

But still I waited on him as on any other; something within me it is true seemed to say I was a hypocrite. Should not I myself perish if I persisted in such a course? I was ashamed myself of the kind words I had to say, and always had a feeling as though I were unclean —unwashed. I got no more real sleep, I was dissatisfied with everything and a burthen to myself.

One day the house-steward came and brought a letter; the Captain asked who read the patient's letters, and the steward said he himself was a trustworthy person.

"Good, first read me the signature."

"Bergschinder. A singular name!"

"Aye and there is not such another rascal in the world. Read the letter, and Gitta, you can stay—I have no more secrets."

There was much in the letter that we did not understand. Schaller wrote that it could not yet be fixed when he should arrive, and the end ran somewhat to this effect.

"Think yourself lucky that you are quit of the dragon. Your eyes are bound, but you will not be led astray but guided into a new and jolly life."

The Captain laughed a forced laugh, then he asked me if I could read well; I said I could, and then he decided on having his letters read by me for the future; he had confidence in me. I had also to read books to him; at villainous tricks which filled me with horror he would often call out:

"That is splendid! what clever rascals, to be sure!"

I read him too a story of a blood-revenge, and he thought everything that occurred in it quite a matter of course.

Only once did he speak of the wife who had abandoned him. It came about in this way. When the Princess left the establishment she gave a farewell concert or entertainment, I hardly know which to call it, it was beautiful. The Princess played magnificently on the harp, and in gratitude for being so far cured she wished to play in the grand saloon to all the patients who could be allowed to leave their rooms. The Professor sent me to the Princess. The whole thing was not without danger, for the beautiful music might stir and affect them so much as to make them cry, and so do them much mischief. A very careful selection was therefore made. Seldom have any folks been made more happy by music. There sat men and women, old and young; they could not see each other but they all could hear the sweet sounds that go so tenderly to the heart. One poor lout who had never even dreamed of such a thing in his whole life suddenly exclaimed at a soft passage:

"I am in Heaven! the angels in Heaven must make such music."

Excepting this little interruption all went well.

The Captain too was invited, but he refused with vehemence, and said:

"I will never hear the sound of a harp again; she"—and he meant his wife—"used to play the harp."

CHAPTER XXX.

THE assistant surgeon who, as I have said, had been in the army, told me the history of the Captain. I must call him the Captain, although he was so no longer. Just as every soldier must come to drill clean and in perfect order so it is throughout and in everything; the officers will not have any man among them, who has a spot on his honour; it affects the honour and dignity of all.

The Captain had married a very proud and beautiful girl; he always must have the best of everything, and it was said she did not care for him; why, no one knew—perhaps because she could not really care for any one. He thought, however, that if he spent a great deal of money on her, and gave her everything she could wish, by that he should win her to love him. And so he sacrificed his honour and his conscience,

14*

and at last robbed others of their property and
life to win his wife's affection. But love is not
to be bought, and the man who tries to win it
in that way does not deserve it. The assistant
could still pity the captain, I could not. If his
wife could not bear him, could he not take her
as she was or let her alone? He might then
have preserved some respect at any rate—but
as it was!—

What the beginning of it all was, the assistant did not know. The Captain kept splendid
horses—he and his wife used often to ride out,
and folks would stand by the road and gaze
after them—he spent a great deal on his horses,
buying and selling and betting heavily as well.
May-be that either in these transactions or in
his professional service something went wrong;
no one knew what it was, but one fine day the
Captain asked leave to resign his commission
and obtained it.

He had run his horses in races everywhere
—I don't know where not — and had won a
great deal of money.

But one day it all came to light. The officers had for a long time disliked his putting himself forward so much—the Captain here and the Captain there, always the Captain—and his wife herself drove, and never less than four horses. So they watched him narrowly, and at last they caught him. The jockey who rode a famous horse in one of the great races on which very heavy stakes were laid, fell from his horse just short of the winning-post, and then it all came out. The jockey confessed that the Captain had bribed him, and then a private enquiry was held; the Captain was turned out and disgraced; he was no longer to style himself Captain and might think himself lucky that he was not brought before a court of justice.

If this favour had not been shown him my father would never have been reduced to beggary. And this too was the reason why he had told father not to call him Captain but by his name, Baron von Haueisen. Ronymus had known something of this business at the time when my father turned him away, but not all,

and at that time the Captain picked the quarrel,
so that he might drag my father into a rotten
business and leave him to be ruined. True it
was that the man was hardly punished; his
wife had forsaken him, and he was going
blind; but he deserved more, a thousand times
more.

I learnt the same lesson as the doctor's
widow, but in a different way. It is written no
doubt: 'Love your enemies.' But man cannot
do it—let no one tell me that he can; the saying cannot have been meant so. Do good to
your enemy—that you can do; but no one need
tell me that even that is easy. If your enemy
is beggared you can give him money and help
him up; you give away what belongs to you,
but you yourself remain the same. But to
watch him every hour, to have perfect patience,
and speak gently, and comfort him—I know
what it is—and no one who has not tried it
himself, knows what it is and need not speak as
if he did. Nay, and it came to worse than
this; for the hardest of all is when the work

which has hitherto brought happiness, and has
been regarded as a task set by God himself
which it was a joy to fulfil, is embittered and
marred. I was tormented with the thoughts:
'Why must there be such a thing as sick-
nursing? Why is it laid on me of all people?
I have had enough of it; I will go away, go
where the world is gayer than here.' Aye—
I felt I was unfaithful, and I had to take my
heart in both hands, as our saying is, to be
able to come to my right mind again, and
not to tear myself free from the man who
had ruined my father and me. And even
then I still meant to go to the Professor,
and tell him I could not attend on that
man.

I was already standing at the door of the
Professor's room when I stood still, and said
to myself: 'No, I know myself what I
ought to do and what I must do, and I will
prove it.' I turned away, and went back to
my duty.

And I did my duty as if he were any other

man of whom I knew nothing except that he was blind.

But I had expected too much of my-self.

———

CHAPTER XXXI.

I FULFILLED my pledge to the end—no, to within one step of the end. It is hard to tell about—but I must tell you—

The Captain wanted to know from the Professor whether he was sure of the cure, and he asked a great many questions; at last the Professor said:

. "Ask no more questions; what I have to tell you I will say of my own accord; and you are a man—"

"And a soldier who can look danger in the face. I am firm—only promise me you will not give me chloroform."

"That I will not, I repeat; the operation is in my hands, the chances of recovery are in yours. So long as you are so violent and excitable I cannot operate; you must learn first to be calm and patient that you may practise it afterwards. So show your courage by patience and submissiveness."

I had never heard the Professor speak so severely to any patient as he did to the Captain. He knew why it was.

One day I was called down into the hall, and who should I find but Ronymus, trembling in every limb and unable to utter a word. At last he said :

"I have heard that the Captain is here in your establishment. The servant who brought him here is with us as waiter. Ah! The Almighty knows where to let the thunder fall. The Captain is bad, but there must have been a worse to visit his sins upon him. God sent him his wife, and He can send devils as well; she has left him, she took a deal of money and went off with another man. And the best joke of all, is, that he still thinks of her and would take her back again. I will tell you one thing; when the Captain comes out again I will let him know who I am."

"How?"

"He must restore what he robbed from your father, and you, the princess of Schlehenhof, shall not be a servant any more."

"Give over, with your 'princess.' Listen to reason; if the Captain were to give back everything could he restore my father to life."

"No—that he cannot. But the money—"

"No one can compel him."

"May be—but do you give me notice when he leaves, and he shall learn what these can do."

He doubled his fists, but he smiled when I opened his hands and asked him to promise that he would never trouble himself any farther about the Captain.

"Have you seen him yet?" he asked; I hastily answered that I was in a hurry. I could not tell Ronymus somehow, just then, that it was my special duty to attend to the miserable man.

When I was alone again I felt just as if some one was stretching out a hand to shelter

me; I was protected and safe, there was a man
within reach whom I could call upon for help
like an affectionate brother. I had many, of
course, who were kind to me; but a faithful
friend from childhood, that is a different thing
again—he has the same love for everything at
home as one has oneself. That I cared at that
time for Ronymus as a woman loves her husband I cannot say. I saw well enough how it
was with him, but it was not so with me.
When the Captain was gone again I should have
borne the worst that could happen; everything
else would be easy to me, and I would stay
there all my life.

Ronymus, dear good soul, he would get used
to it. It was hard, but it must be.

CHAPTER XXXII.

IT was the Saturday before that Sunday—
the Professor had been obliged to set out across
country early in the morning and would not
return till late in the evening—when I had a
visit from my brother-in-law at Rheinfeld. He
said he had business in the place, and could not
go away without hunting me out, although for
years I had not thought of Agnes and much
less of him and his belongings. I was obliged
to confess myself wrong; I myself could not
understand how, in my constant anxiety for the
patients, I had let myself forget every one
else.

"But now for that very reason take a rest,"
said my brother-in-law. "You look very bad;
quite different to what I should have expected.
You are over-straining yourself. Come to us
for a few weeks, and rest and make yourself

happy. We love you and esteem you, besides
you owe it to Agnes to look after her a little;
you are her mother's only sister — rest her
soul!"

What was this? A hand stretched down
from Heaven to set me free from my misery.

"Don't take too long to consider," my
brother-in-law insisted. "Why in this house it
is just as if the sun never shone; I cannot
think how you can bear to stay here. With us
at any rate in a few weeks you will soon have
your red cheeks again. Speak to your Professor—he must give you leave. Or shall I
speak to him instead of you?"

I had to explain that the Professor was
absent, and would not return till late in the
evening.

"Then I will stay the night here," said my
brother-in-law, "and to-morrow will be Sunday
and we will set out together—you know, like
that time when you got quite cheerful again,
and forgot a peck of troubles and sorrows.
Why, the whole village, the whole neighbour-

hood will rejoice when you come; we often and often talk about you. Down in Heyden there, things are not what they were in your time and in the time of the famous Doctor—I read in the paper that he was dead. The fruit-merchant at Rorschach, he is dead too. You may be glad that you did not marry him; you would be a widow now with a heap of children; but the Colonel from Sträussle is still alive, he comes to see us and often asks after you. Oh! we shall all be delighted to see you and particularly Agnes, and my other children remember you too, and sing the songs you taught them."

Pure peace, and liberty, air and sunshine rose up before me as my brother-in-law spoke, and it all seemed to fit in so beautifully; while I was away the Captain might leave the establishment, and need never know who had nursed him; I lived in terror of the hour when he would see me and thank me—No, he should never see me, never thank me.

I sat silent, but breathing hard, and my

brother-in-law went on to say how it was said that my skill was quite famous, that I was the Professor's regular assistant, and that I had a fixed share of the payment for each cure; this I had to contradict and deny.

"Still you must have laid by a good bit of money?" asked my brother-in-law. I did not hesitate to tell him the sum, and that the Professor had laid it by for me in the Savings Bank. He, however, found my savings far below his expectations; he added that the Savings Bank gave far too low interest, and he thereupon went on to say that he was wanting to make an addition to his house, that he did not care to draw money out of the business, because it brought him a better return to leave it there, but if I would hand the money I had laid by over to him, he would give me a mortgage on the house and double interest. I told him that I never would have anything to do with money matters; I had had enough to suffer from them in my young days.

"Aye, indeed—" said he promptly. "I daresay now. You are thinking that I mean to make you pay for what your father lost me? It never came into my head. How could you help that? You would have more than enough to do if you set to work to set that straight. No, that is no concern of yours; and your father himself had none of it—that scoundrel of a Captain robbed him of it all."

There again!—The man who was lying in there—whom I had to wait upon and help, had not only robbed my father; he had also misled him into bringing loss on others.

"There now, you look so sad all of a sudden," said my brother-in-law, "that I am quite grieved that I spoke to you of money matters at all. Take it as unsaid and forget it; my hand upon it, I will never mention a word about them again. Leave your money in the Savings Bank. You are quite right. But I will not give in about your coming home with me; you must come or else you will be thinking I came about the money. I can borrow it

wherever I choose; and you shall see we love
and care for you as a sister."

He spoke warmly and out of an honest
heart; but it was past and over. The talk
about money seemed suddenly to have strewn
ashes over everything; I would have nothing to
do with the outside world, I would stay here at
my post, come what might.

I begged my brother-in-law to send Agnes
to me, and I would pay the expenses of her
journey. He replied that he would take an
opportunity of bringing her and rose to go. I
told him that Ronymus was living at Baur on
the Lake, and that he should go to see him;
he answered that he would not take three steps
out of his way to see the road-mender's son; I
kept myself, however, from reproving his ar-
rogance. And so our parting was far less
affectionate than our meeting had been, although as we shook hands at last my brother-
in-law repeated his hope that I might soon pay
him a visit. As soon as he was gone it struck
me that I ought to have sent Agnes something;

I might have sent her the Captain's chain. But no, she should wear no remembrance of the man who had ruined her grandfather.

I heard the whistle of the engine of the train that carried my brother-in-law homewards. How good it would have been if it could have carried me away too. But what had to be, had to be—

That very night before the Captain's eyes were operated on, the lady died who had cried herself blind. The Captain was sleeping soundly; the Professor and his assistant came noiselessly down stairs; in the house all was still.

———

CHAPTER XXXIII.

THE preparations for an operation were really much more trying to the patients than the operation itself. The Captain had demanded to be told the day, and the Professor had consented. When the Captain woke early in the morning he called me, and asked:

"Is it day yet?"

"It is dawning."

"To-day then it will be decided whether I ever see daylight again, or live in eternal night."

He asked for something to eat, and when I told him that he might not eat anything beforehand he laughed loudly, and said:

"What, I must learn to fast too!" Then he lay silent, and at last he said to himself:

"Well, I have a quiet conscience. What

are you sighing for?" he.shouted out suddenly.
I had to keep myself from crying out: 'You—
you robber and murderer; how can you talk of
a quiet conscience?'

The Captain was conducted downstairs, and
submitted to everything without a sound. Our
Professor gave him chloroform, and as I saw
him lying there, still and lifeless, such a strange
feeling came over me — but now I must not
think of anything but business, I must be
ready to hand everything, and take everything.

"When are you going to begin?" said the
Captain in a faint voice.

"It is all done, and now only be quiet, perfectly quiet," said the Professor.

"Is Gitta there? Give me your hand, Gitta,"
said the Captain in a strangely soft voice. I
gave him my hand, and I can honestly say I
wished with my whole heart that his cure might
be complete. All hatred and wrath had been
taken out of my soul. Aye, I hoped he might
recover his sight and do well. To be sure he

could not bring my father back to life—but I
could not think of that just then.

When the Captain was carried back to his
room again, he asked, 'why the piano was not
being played overhead as usual.'

The Professor gave me a sign, and answered
that there would not be any more music now,
that the piano was going to be sent away; and
he went hastily out of the room. The Captain
asked for Rack; the good beast had known he
would soon be wanted; to-day for the first time
he went up to the Captain without being called,
and laid down his head for the suffering man
to put his hand on it.

The Captain soon fell asleep, Rack gently
drew his head away and came to lie in front of
me, making believe to be asleep; but he often
winked up at me. I could not help wondering
once more how it was possible that the dog
should know everything in this way? But Rack
shook his head as much as to say, 'It is of no
use puzzling yourself; you will never make it
out, any more than I could bring out the words

which I should like to say to you.' But if at
that moment the dog had begun to speak I
should not have been a bit astonished, and
when I took him by the cars and stroked him,
he twitched his lips as if he wished to smile,
and was sorry that he could not.

Presently the Captain woke, and asked how
long it was since he had been operated on. I
told him he had been asleep a good hour; he
spoke with great appreciation of how skilfully
and easily the Professor had done it, and I, on
the other hand, could tell him of the great
Berlin Doctor, of whom he had learnt it.

I, in my simplicity, went on telling him
about the great Doctor and pouring out my
whole heart; but in the middle of my story I
saw I had not done wisely in telling this to
this man; still, I talked on, as if I could not
help it. Meanwhile too I thought; 'if he hears
what holy men there are in the world he
will be converted in soul, and follow better
ways.'

He did not say a word to it all, and I asked

him if he would not like something to eat; he said he should. I rang the bell, and just as the maid-servant brought in the food there was a noise overhead of trampling feet and of moving furniture.

"What is that?" asked the Captain. "What is it? Is the roof coming in on my head; is the house being pulled down?"

The girl said: "It is nothing more than that they are carrying down the body of the lady who cried her eyes out."

I was in despair at the idiotic girl's saying it out in this way, but I added quickly:

"Eat something now?"

"Go away—go!" shrieked the Captain, and he flung everything on to the floor where it fell in a smash, and then he turned over. That was just what he ought not to do; he ought not to move at all.

I sent for the Professor, and he said that in this case it was of no consequence; but I did not know what that could mean.

Towards evening the Captain woke again, and asked for food. I gave it him, and he said : .

"But -it is not true. No, there is no love——"

———.

CHAPTER XXXIV.

IT is always best when the first bandage can be kept on as long as possible; in this case, however, it soon had to be removed, and as the Professor did it he said to me that I could very well do it single-handed for the future. He said this in a way quite different from his usual manner. I did not know whether I judged rightly, but it seemed to me that the Professor had quite a different way with him from what he usually had; it was as if he had no real heart in the Captain's case, and no true liking for him, and had to put a strong curb on himself.

One day, just as I had fastened on a fresh bandage the house-steward brought in Schaller, and with him came too a man, who had been a forester over a small district.

In the years since I had last seen Berg-

schinder, he had very much altered and grown
very stout, but his clean shaved face still looked
just as if pure universal benevolence were always at home there, and he smacked his tongue
just as he used to do, as if he had a lollypop
in his mouth.

The Captain called out to the forester:

"Go away—you reek of wine!"

"The Captain does not like the smell of
wine, because he must not drink it at present,"
said Schaller laughing, as he seated himself in
a large chair, and unbuttoned his waistcoat over
his big stomach.

"Well, my noble Captain," said he. "Am
not I a splendid fellow? Don't I keep my word?
Hey—what?"

He always ended with 'Hey—what?' so that
one had to answer him. The Captain begged
Schaller to question the Professor as to how he
was going on, for he would say nothing to him.
Schaller warned his old comrade to be patient,
and preached at him like a parson, and he
made a sign to the forester to pay attention,

and see what a fool he could make of the Captain. Suddenly he interrupted himself to ask who I might be. The Captain replied that he never enquired about the family and circumstances of his servants, for in that case he should have to look after them in times of trouble.

"Here's a fine gentleman! Your true fine gentleman!" cried Schaller. "There is always something to be learnt from a gentleman." As he came close up to me and inspected me I could have clawed his eyes out—but I kept still.

Schaller now went on to talk of losing and winning, and of law-suits that had arisen out of such matters ; then came long stories which I did not understand, but they laughed at them together so loudly and so much, that I had to interfere and say that the patient must not laugh so violently, that it would do him harm, and that he must keep quieter.

Who can tell whether the scoundrels may not have had some suspicion who I was ; the two strangers looked at me with astonishment, and the Captain said:

"Well, we will be quiet.—Come Schaller, be quiet. In this house you must learn to be as quiet as mice. Stay here, Gitta—we will be quieter."

And they went on talking to each other. I looked out at the sky, and could not help thinking: 'Oh merciful God! Thou must know why Thy sun is permitted to shine on these men, and Thou must know why Thou hast given them understanding to enable them to rob their fellowmen.'

I scarcely listened any more, and I shuddered as if hell had been opened before me to look into, when the rascals told each other of their villainous tricks. I heard them speak of Aussichtler, and I now learned his history more exactly. This man, who had been a clock-case maker, lived happily on his lonely hill with his lovely wife; Schaller had cast his eye on the wife, and her husband came in one day just when Schaller wanted to embrace her, and hus-

band and wife together had given Schaller a
good taste of the stick. And what did Schaller
do? He said he would punish the man much
more than any judge would. He sent gentlemen and ladies—even the Captain had been up
there — he told the man beforehand that his
house was in the loveliest situation in all the
country-side, and had the finest view and the
purest air—that some one must certainly build
a country-house there. The simple man believed him; his brain was quite turned, and his
wife died in misery.

Once more I could not help looking up to
Heaven: Why did not a fiery scourge fall from
Heaven and punish these men? I would not
hear any more.

But stay! Now they were talking of my
father. I knew well enough that they had
brought him to ruin, but how it had been
done I now learnt for the first time.

They had first beguiled him with his soldier's pride, and they persuaded him he was

one of the cleverest of men, a real knowing fellow, and that what was most cunning about him was his pretending to be so simple. First they let him make a certain profit, then lose a good part of it, then win still more—and then they had him fast.

Oh! how can I tell you all? I myself scarcely remember it now. Only this one thing. It was exactly as Schmaje had said; Schaller had let himself be overreached by father, and that had been the finishing stroke. That my father should have been ruined was hard enough, but that he should have been brought to it by treachery was still the hardest. And the Captain laughed again at this mean stratagem! Then the forester said:

"There must still be a child of Xander's living. Does no one know what is become of her?"

Schaller said he had heard that the girl had gone to her brother-in-law in Switzerland, and had grown remarkably hand-some.

"When I am well again I will look her up," said the Captain.

"You are right," said Schaller. "You are, as I may say, a single man again. Money, to be sure, you cannot give her, but your life is a good one, you can insure it—" And they laughed again; what at I don't know, and to this day I cannot tell how I held myself quiet.

The men went away. This was enough —I could hear no farther. I was fully de-termined; not a minute longer would I stay with the Captain, I would go to the Pro-fessor, and tell him everything. As I went out of the door Rack was lying at the threshold, which was what he never had done before, he had always come straight in to me; but I make no doubt the beast knew full well what villains these were, and would not come in. While I stood still, thinking

this, the Captain called me in a voice full
of anguish, but with all his might.   I
could do nothing else, but go in to him
again.

CHAPTER XXXV.

THE Captain was standing upright in the middle of the room shouting:

"Gitta, Gitta, where are you?"

"Here I am."

"It is pricking like a thousand needles. Make haste and loosen the bandage."

He sat down, I stood before him; I could not say a word, I felt as if I were being strangled—but I loosened the bandage, and he said:

"When I am well I will make you a handsome present."

"I should not take anything—from you certainly, nothing."

"From me! and why not? why not from me?"

"My mother, God rest her, was right when she said, one might be strangled with a gold chain."

"What - are you saying? What does this mean?"

"I will tell you — I am Xander's daughter."

I had the bandage in my hand; he screamed and flung himself upon me; I shrieked and the dog flew at the Captain. I snatched away the bandage—

"There look at me—see me first."

He screamed out: "Blind! blind! Xander!" and fell on the floor.

I left him lying there and ran away—whither I knew not. I could still hear a voice behind me, screaming: 'Xander! Xander!' I ran downstairs, and hid myself first in the wood-shed.

Where should I go? I did not know. 'Blind, blind! Xander, Xander!' rang out from every stone in the wall. What had happened? what had I done? I had revenged myself—I

16*

had blinded my enemy. I knelt prostrate, and I felt as if I had been flung into a great gulf where waters surged below me, and the rocks above me began to roll down upon me.

I heard running and calling in the house. Aye, it was all over. All the well-doing of years wiped out in one instant; I had done worse than murder; I had no right to live. I knew the way out of the woodshed into the street; I forced open the door and ran out. Down there was the Lake. Into the Lake with you, murderess, worse than murderess!

I ran down the street. Under the electric clock I paused and took breath—it was five o'clock, my last hour. As I started off running again a man took hold of me, and said:

"How glad I am to see you again, Gitta. But what makes you look so distracted? What is the matter with you? Can I help you in any way?"

It was the Professor of astronomy; he held

me firmly by the arm; I tried to tear myself away, but he said:

"My child, my good child"—Oh! how it struck to my heart—"My good child, regard me as your father."

"My father! my father! I have taken revenge for my father."

"What are you talking about?"

"Leave go of me."

"Child, I am an old man. Don't make me struggle here with you in the street. See, the folks are looking at us."

"What do I care for the folks?"

"You are hurting me—I am not strong enough to hold you."

"I do not want to hurt you—good-bye, good-bye."

I tore myself away and ran on; down in the plain I stood still. It was Sunday, ever so many folks, men and women, were out taking their pleasure—I would not spoil their happiness; if I were to jump into the water here I

should soon be pulled out again—down there
by the Schänzeli, there I would leap over the
parapet when the steamboat put off, and the
wash would bury me at once. Some boys were
sitting on the disused crane by the Winkelried-
haus and spinning merrily round and round;
out beyond shone the white houses and the
green, vine-covered hills; bright sails skimmed
over the Lake, pleasure parties were being
carried hither and thither—I saw it all, but I was
thinking of something quite different—I was in
quite another spot. I was up in the wood
where the trees had been felled, that night with
my father. We were sitting outside the village,
waiting for day, and freezing—

Then and there I longed for vengeance:
Now I had had my revenge, now it was enough
—away with life.—

I went on the bridge over the Schänzeli,
and there Ronymus met me, saying:

"It is well that you are at liberty for once.
I must go down to the boat; just be so good as
to hold this wallet for me, there are things

in it of great value. I will be back in a moment."

He was gone, and I held the wallet in my
hand. I stood there and saw how the boat put
off; on board there were such a number of
folks in their Sunday clothes and music was
playing. 'Are there men among those, who
have done what you have done?—Away with
you, you blinder of men!' The waves splashed
on the bank, why did I not spring into the
waters. What do I care for the wallet and the
valuables? What do I care for the whole
world? To whom do all the gold and silver
and woods and forests in the world belong?
They may fight for them when I am dead—

I saw Ronymus coming, and suddenly a
light flashed upon my soul. 'Die—why dying
is nothing. Nay, you would have it that *he*
should make amends for the ill he had done
— and you?   Would you escape?   Nay,
back you must go, and repent and make
amends—'

I flung the wallet to Ronymus, and ran

back to the establishment. I had to struggle
through the crowd that were coming towards
me as if I were swimming against the waves of
the Lake.

CHAPTER XXXVI.

WHEN I went into the house Rack leaped up on me, and was rejoiced to see me back again. Then he lay humbly down as if to show me that he knew he was guilty as well as I. I sent to tell the Professor I was there, and he desired that I should wait for him in the operating-room. There I had to stay a long time in solitude; I gazed at the large printed placards and at two words in particular which were on the wall: 'Patience. Hope.' These were set before the patients operated upon to see if they could read them. I read the words, I saw the letters. How much might be spelt into these letters, how much might be made out of them—but what I had to say never had anything to do with them.

At last the Professor rang for me to go to him; he was sitting at his writing-table writing. Without looking up at me he said:

"Sit down," and went on writing. At last he turned to me, and said:

"I was sure you would come back again, and I did not send to look for you. We must make no scandal for the credit and dignity of the house."

At last I brought out these words :

"Aye, I have sinned not only against the man himself but against your whole household. May I be allowed to ask how the Captain is going on now?"

The Professor took off his spectacles, breathed upon them, rubbed them bright, laid them down again, and said in a voice which was quite strange to me:

"Aye, indeed, you may well ask. There was a good deal of blood lost, but he is pretty well again now."

"And is he blind?"

"Yes."

"And will remain blind?"

"Yes."

I felt as if I could not breathe, nor ever raise my eyes again; but I collected myself and told how it had all happened. The Professor remained silent for a long time. At last he said, without looking at me:

"It was not right in you not to have told me long ago what the Captain had done to you. Still, what you meant to do was base and cruel. Now, I have every confidence that you will obey my commands."

"In everything, everything. What shall I do?"

"At present nothing whatever. Go to your own room, and do not quit it till I desire you. I rely upon you to attempt nothing without my knowledge. Go to your room, lock the door, and open it to no one but me; or, better still, I will lock you in. Give me your hand and word that you will behave quietly."

I gave him my hand, and his, usually so steady and calm, was trembling. He led me to my room, and locked the door upon me.

There I sat, a prisoner. I opened my trunk, I don't know why. There were my savings and my clothes, and there lay the chain.

"Oh mother! mother! how could you have foreseen it?"

I sat a long time on my trunk; my thoughts were with the dead lying out there, out of the world, and it was a relief to my heart that at last I could cry.

The evening chimes rang up from the town, the folks were returning now from their Sunday excursions, rejoicing in the rest of falling night and in the labour of to-morrow; and I— what would become of me? Should I be taken into a court for trial, and have to repent for years? A prisoner turns over every word that has been said to him a hundred times. The Professor had distinctly said he would make no fuss, no scandal, that the dignity of the house required that—then he would not hand me over to justice; but what then would happen to me? How should I be punished? I would take it patiently whatever it might be and repent.

Why had the Professor said what I meant to do?—Meant? had I not done it then? Had I only dreamed that I had done it, and had he not said that he would always be blind?

There was a scratching at the door; good old Rack wanted to come in to me, but he could not get in and he whined pitifully. Ah! never as long as I lived could I take any pleasure again in man or beast.

What would the doctor's widow say when she heard it? and Ronymus? Ah! that good Ronymus, that faithful soul; it would grieve him to the heart that I should be such a thing —no one in the world cared for me as he did. And then in the midst of my wretchedness it rose up in my heart that I loved him, loved him truly, and I could not help crying for him and for myself. I had begged and persuaded him to do no harm to the Captain, and now I had done it myself, and such a horrible thing! I cried out loud for grief.

I heard every quarter strike from the towers in the town below, and once I flung open the window and felt as if I must throw myself out, but I had promised the Professor to do nothing without telling him; certainly he had meant that I should not destroy my own life.

And down below lay the Captain in night that would never have an end. Suddenly I felt as if in myself a new day had dawned. Aye— that was it—and so it should be! I vowed to myself that I would never leave the Captain as long as he lived; I would take care of him as if he were my father, and thank God if He would inflict on me no worse punishment.

I opened the window; a shooting star flew across the sky as if to show me a sign that my offering was accepted. God be praised and thanked, there was still some good that I could do—

I lay down and perceived that I was dreadfully hungry, but in the room there was nothing but water; I drank some, thinking how I had wanted to drown myself. Nay, nay, I was still living and must still live and do some good. Then I went to sleep and did not wake till I heard a knocking at my door.

———

CHAPTER XXXVII.

IT was the Professor who said:

"I know you must have passed a bitter night; in this one night you have lived through seven years of imprisonment; you deserved it. But now I can give you some comfort: You did not blind the Captain."

"What do you say? Is he well then, can he see?"

"Be calm and let me speak. I had from the first but little hope, still I thought there was a possibility of cure, but as soon as the operation was over it was decisive; so be comforted. As you yourself must see you cannot stay with me any longer, but you shall not be turned out of the house. Stay here until something suitable opens up for you. I am writing to the doctor's widow, perhaps she will have

some advice to offer or may take you to be
with her."

Oh! if the joys of heaven were suddenly
offered to, a condemned soul, he could not be
happier than I was. But I told the Professor
at once that I had determined never to quit
the Captain, but to stay with him if he would
have me. I was still guilty—I had intended to
do it.

The Professor looked at me in astonishment,
but with a clear bright gaze; he was for some
time silent as was his way. Then he cautioned
me not to be overhasty, he could not altogether
approve of my plan, and besides it had to be
considered whether the Captain might not fly
at me in his fury. That I had not considered,
but still I thought that there would be no
danger of that; a blind man is feeble, and I
was strong, and I would conquer him by gen-
tleness. I asked whether the Captain understood that I was not the cause of his blindness,
and the Professor said that he had called him a
bungler and abused him in even worse terms.

I asked to be allowed to go to the Captain, and I begged to be let go to him alone, but this the Professor would not agree to.

We went together to the Captain. He sat bent forwards in the large armchair, his hand lay on Rack's head. He did not stir when he heard us go in. When the Professor said: "Gitta is here and wishes to ask your forgiveness," he pushed the dog aside, sat upright, and said "Indeed? And is that to be the end of it? I expect a telegram from my friend Schaller—a lawyer shall teach you what is due to me and to you. Now Gitta, are you satisfied with your vengeance?"

Before I could reply the Professor repeated that my action was a base infraction of duty, but that in any case his sight could not have been saved. The Captain muttered something unintelligible to himself, and then he cried out:

"Bah! I am caught in a den of rogues and hypocrites; but I am not yet quite clear about your tricks and dodges—was she to pull off

the bandage in order that your bungling might
not be discovered, or are you ready to acknowledge yourself a bungler for the sake of white-
washing this hussy, who was such a favourite
with your great Berlin Doctor?"

I shuddered, for it was as if some one spoke
from the bottommost hell. This was how this
wretch could distort and befoul everything?
How sad! The man was so miserable and so
venomous.

I collected myself, and told him that I
should not let myself be put out by hard
words, that I confessed myself guilty; that in
my rage I had meant to blind him, and that I
would make amends for my sin in all humility,
and would serve him and never leave him so
long as he lived.

"You will? Come here, give me your hand,
come closer!" cried the Captain. I gave him
my hand, and he squeezed it till I thought he
would have crushed it.

"I have your promise; you are witness—

17*

you, Professor," he snarled out. I pulled away my hand, and said:

"You have hurt me, and it must be the last time this happens. I tell you I will keep my promise; but note well that I am stronger than you, and if you ever again illtreat me, be it how it may, I will leave you that very hour. Those are my conditions."

All was still in the room; a letter was brought in. The Captain desired me to read it, and it was to say that Schaller had died of apoplexy, with the champagne glass that he had just emptied still in his hand. The Captain bit his lip hard but he did not utter a sound. When the Professor rose to go, he said:

"Stay awhile, Professor. I require one thing more of you, and then I renounce everything."

"What do you require?"

"Give me poison. What have I to live for?"

"I fully expected you to make this demand, but you must have told yourself beforehand that I should not accede to it. You gentlemen always expect us to look on life as a duty, while for you it is to be nothing but enjoyment; a pleasant draught or, failing that, you break the vessel. You do not wish to live any longer, but you must live, and you will be thankful for it yet."

"Shall I? Good. I will lay your noble sentiments to heart," sneered the Captain, half agreeing but half annoyed.

The Professor left us, I remained with the Captain; he called me to him and said that in his valise there was a double barrelled pistol, loaded; I was to get it for him—he must shoot himself, he could not live, and he exacted my obedience as the one and only expiation for my wrong-doing. My heart stood still but I controlled myself, and asked him:

"Who will ensure me that you will shoot yourself and not me?"

"Ah! indeed, you are extremely prudent; well, lay the pistol on the table in front of me, and leave the room."

I told him that I would do nothing of the kind, and he impressed upon me urgently that I was exacting too much from myself; that it was impossible that I should nurse him, and wait upon him, I could not help cursing him.

"And even if you really are kind to me what should I live for?"

Heaven inspired me with the right thing to say:

"You must live in order that I may do some good for you." That settled him; his features twitched and he trembled all over.

"You good to me? I will believe it. Then I am to live that good may be done to me!"

He lay down and soon was fast asleep.

CHAPTER XXXVIII.

I WAS sitting in the next room when I was informed that a man from my own home would take no refusal but said he must speak with me. Who could it be? I hurried down into the hall, and there stood the road-mender, Ronymus' father.

"Do you know me again?" he said with a grin. "I look quite another man, don't I? Ronymus has dressed me out and got me up, and had new clothes made for me. But come into the parlour, I have something to say to you, something pleasant."

In the parlour the good man could not cease wondering at my having altered so much; one minute he said I was just like my father, and the next I was just like my mother. At last he came to the conclusion that in figure I was like my father, and in face like my mother, only my forehead nose and mouth were my father's. I could not help laughing, and was fairly astonished to find I could still laugh.

I begged him to speak low as I had a patient close by who was asleep.

"Aye—it is well you should remind me of my principal business. There must be an end put to this sick-nursing. We will not let you do it any longer. You, the daughter of Schleh-hof! No, this must not go on any longer. If only *she* had lived to see it; she loved you as dearly as if she had borne you in her bosom. Aye, let me cry a bit, it does me no harm, I hope some one will cry for me when I am gone. Now—for fear I should forget it—before she died she made me swear that I would hand you over the money from your half of the goat and your three half-geese. I have it with me; and there are the descendants of your cocks and hens, I will take them to you at the Lamb Inn.

I did not understand what all this could mean, and it was difficult to bring the good man to the point. When I asked him what he meant by the Lamb Inn, he cried out:

"What? don't you know about it yet? You must know that great busy inn down in the valley; Schmaje found it out, it was his last stroke of business; and there are fields, and pasture with it, and a plot of vineyard and a bit of forest; everything, everything, and all the household chattels are there too, there is nothing to buy; there you may live together in plenty and comfort. So Ronymus has not told you yet anything about his having bought the 'Lamb' and that you and he are to keep the inn together? And I shall be there too, I am going with him. I still can work enough to earn my victuals, and it is always well to have someone belonging to you in an inn who can keep an eye on things, and see that there is no waste, and no cheating. Servants are good for nothing now-a-days, but I will look after yours for you." The road-mender saw the portrait of the great oculist on the wall, and he turned to address him as if he were a Saint.

"Ah! you who could restore sight—you will be glad too to see us all together. Brigitta, we will give that picture the best place in the house, and your children after you shall be taught to remember that man."

I had let the old man talk on as far as this, and if before I had felt as if the Captain spoke from the depths of hell, I felt now as if the good old man spoke down from heaven; that was the feeling that came over me. And he thought all would yet go well; but it was too late—it was all over now. I asked after Ronymus, and his father laughed.

"He—he is clean out of his wits, that is to say he is in his senses in everything else, that he has proved by saving so much, but he is clean out of his wits for love of you; it is our way—I was just as bad over Bonifacia. Oh Lord! oh Lord! why could not she have been spared to sing your children to sleep! You know how well she could sing; but now she is singing up in heaven, if we could but hear her." He cried so that he could say no more, and I only said "Aye—master."

"Don't say master—say father-in-law."

"Does Ronymus know about the Captain?"

"Of course—and serve the villain right that he should be blind."

From the next room the Captain called out.

"Who is there? Who says it serves me right?" I begged the road-mender to go now, and to send Ronymus to me in the evening; then I went to the Captain. I had to tell him who it was, and he said in a low voice:

"Every street-sweeper can crow over me now."

CHAPTER XXXIX.

IN the evening came Ronymus; he laid his
hands on his breast, and he could not speak—
I took his hand, led him into my sitting-room,
and said to him.

"Ronymus, you love me, and I will tell you
plainly I love you too, but—"

"What's the 'but'? All is well, nothing
more is needed."

"Nay Ronymus; I still have a heavy burden
on my shoulders."

"I can carry you though you still had seven
hundred weight on them," and he lifted me up,
and carried me round the room in his arms, as
if I were a mere child. I had to beg him to
set me down again; he did so and I said:

"Ronymus, I have taken a solemn vow of
repentance. The Captain is blind for ever—not
by my fault—that is by God's mercy—but I

wished and meant to blind him, I must atone for that."

"That is cutting it too fine," Ronymus remonstrated. "Think you—if every one were to set to work to atone for the things he has wished to do the whole world would be a house of correction, and there would be no one to superintend it even. God Almighty himself would have to turn governor of a penitentiary. I cannot believe it—but even supposing you did wish to blind the Captain, it is all the same now as if you had not; you are not guilty, and why will you not take the benefit of it since he must have been blind any way?"

"I have promised him."

"Stop! that promise does not now hold good; a servant who marries is free from his bond by law. I will talk to the man, and he must give you up of his own free will or we will compel him by law."

"But even if he gave me up freely, believe me I could never forgive myself if I left him;

I could never be happy for one single hour—
neither for you nor for myself."

"That is nonsense—you must be happy."

"Ronymus, I have solemnly promised the
Captain not to quit him as long as I have an
eye to see with."

"Well, well, you shall keep your eyes
seventy-seven years all the same, and a few
Decembers after that again. Aye—so be it
then; we will take the rascal home with us, and
give him his victuals till he dies."

"Nay, Ronymus, that won't do; you must do
it with a good will."

"A man cannot force himself to good will;
but for love of you I can consent. You, I must
have, and you I will take if I am to take seven
devils into the bargain. And, indeed, when I
consider the matter rightly, it will suit very
well; we have an inn with eleven rooms and
five attics, and the Captain must still have a
good lump of money left from the time of his
robbery, and when I consider the matter rightly
a good action never brings evil. Why you will·

make a good-natured fellow of me.—But why are you laughing? why are you crying?"

I could not speak, and Ronymus took both my hands and looked me in the face, and said, it seemed just like a dream to him that the 'Princess of Schlehenhof' would marry him, but still it must be true, and in token that it was true I must give him a kiss. Then I begged him to come with me to the Captain and settle everything. He said: "Aye, aye—it is always the way with me. Once when I was quite a little boy your uncle Donatus' ferocious dog tore my breeches; I carried a nice sharp stone in my pockets for weeks to have a fling at that dog's head, but when I might have done it I took the stone out of my pocket, and did nothing to the dog. And it's just the same now with the Captain. Come along—I will soon make it all right."

So we went to the Captain hand in hand.

"Captain, Sir," said I, "I have brought my betrothed with me."

"What? You? Who? Who do you say?"

He did not let me speak, but cursed and swore
at all the world; he, a blind man, was betrayed
and cheated, and solemn oaths counted for nothing. He flung out his arms, and shrieked out,
if he could but throttle me—one woman for all
the rest.

"Will you listen to us calmly and patiently?" said Ronymus.

"Who speaks—who is that?"

"I—Ronymus."

"And who are you—Ronymus?"

"I was servant at Schlehenhof with Xander;
I offended you then, Sir; please to forgive me
—you need not say so. I hated you then, Sir,
but I don't hate you now. We will treat you
with due respect. Let me speak to the end. I
have been a soldier; but no—that is not what
I meant to say. We have bought an inn, and
you shall live there with us, and be as comfortable as you can, and I and my wife and our
children after us will be your servants as if you
were the grandfather of the family. And my
father, the road-mender, he will be with us too.

You shall see—that is you shall feel, how we will behave to you day and night; and you will have good living at our place; my mother, God rest her soul, has said a hundred times that no one could cook like Brigitta. I am not good at long speeches, Sir, but do you just agree and all will be well."

His voice broke, big drops stood on his forehead; as he wiped them away I could have kissed his hand; but I could do nothing but cry. Ronymus took my hand:

"You should not cry," said he, "you should be happy."

For some time the Captain did not speak. At last he said:

"What is your name?"

"I told you, Ronymus."

"Ronymus. You believe that I have a good deal of money, and you will inherit it ? "

"Aye—we would take it, indeed—and I think we ought."

"Indeed? You think I am in your debt,

because Xander was ruined? Speak out—you think that?"

"Aye, I do."

The Captain was silent again for a long time; he moved the fingers of both hands impatiently in the air, and then he said:

"Come here, Ronymus, come nearer. You seem to me a thorough good fellow. I might make myself uncommonly comfortable with you if I pretended to be rich; but I will not. I will tell you honestly I have nothing left. Do you believe me?"

"No, I don't believe it."

"But so it is. Now, will you be just as glad to take me into your house, and keep me with you?"

"Just as glad?" answered Ronymus, "No. But we will abide by our word; Brigitta says she owes you something, and I as her husband will pay my wife's debts."

"That is good—I trust you. I have been robbed; I have nothing in the world but a good annuity for life. Yes, I will go with you.

Gitta, you will be happy with this man. Gitta, give him my pistols; there is ball in them, Ronymus, but you have been a soldier, you will know how to draw the charges. Now, that will do."

I saw that the Captain's cheeks were flushed, the scar of the old wound on his cheek was scarlet; this ought not to be, he would have another attack of fever; so I told him he must keep quiet, and everything should be settled. Then I went out of the room with Ronymus.

In my own room I threw my arms round his neck, and no woman in this world ever clasped her husband more lovingly than I mine. Is there in all the world a better or a nobler man?

He took something out of his pocket, and said:

"My mother left this to you; it is your token; in this locket is the splinter of stone which was taken out of father's eye, and mother left it to you on her death-bed;

18*

she prophesied that you would become my wife."

When, at last, he went away, he said:

"You, my dear—why I have won Schleh-hof's daughter—I, I have won the Princess of Schlehenhof."

Aye—and to this day Ronymus speaks of my father, and still more of my mother, as if they had been princes, and when he is particularly pleased he calls me—but only between ourselves—the Princess of Schlehenhof.

That night I wrote a letter to the doctor's widow at Montreux. There was one soul in the world to whom I could and must tell everything, and I wrote till my eyes flowed over, and the tears fell on the paper.

CHAPTER XL.

THE parting from the establishment, from our noble Professor, from the patients, and from Rack was a hard one to me. If beasts could cry that good Rack would have cried; when I was packing my trunks I could read in his eyes that he knew I was taking leave for ever.

The doctor's widow had returned to us; she was delighted with Ronymus, and as to the road-mender, she and he were such friends you might have thought they had grown up from childhood together. She gave me a particular pleasure by getting my niece Agnes to come to my wedding. The doctor's widow on one side, and the Professor of astronomy on the other, stood with me before the altar; I felt as if it were my parents.

The road-mender and the Captain came home to the inn here with us. The road-mender was generally good to every one, that is to say, he had not troubled himself much about them, but he had never hurt any one, and bore no ill-will in his heart towards anybody. But he hated the Captain mortally, and at first he would not go with us when he found we were taking the Captain. Ronymus could do nothing with him, but I was more fortunate, and succeeded in making him peaceable at least. I reminded him how he had felt at that time when he had come to Heyden in the dread of losing his eye; and that he should prove his gratitude by being patient with the blind man.

"Aye, when you remind me of that I must need give in," said he.

But never would he do the smallest thing to give the Captain pleasure, and he was always jealous because we and our children showed the man so much respect and ready service. Many a time he would mutter to himself—

"That man in all the days of his life has never worn out a pair of soles that he had earned by honest labour. He has hands as soft as the inside skin of an egg. If either of us had gone blind would he have taken us into house and home?"

It was a hard job to keep the old man always patient; and he was always afraid too lest our children should grow up too genteel, and so he often would say to them, 'Your grandfather was a road-mender, and your father was in service.'

Those good roads which lead from our house, over the hill to the fields and forest, were made by my father-in-law, single-handed. In the house, he looked after everything, and the secret of distilling such capital Kirschwasser Ronymus learnt from his father.

Before I come to the end of my story I
must tell you about Seridja. I had almost forgotten her; whenever I did remember her it
was like a stab in my heart; ingratitude always
returns with a fresh sting. Now, after years
had passed, I had a letter from India, which
had gone first to Zurich, and Seridja wrote to
say that in the hours of pain when her son was
born she could not help remembering how cruel
she had been to me, that she hoped I would
forgive her, and she sent me a beautiful present.

The Captain soon made himself quite at
home with our way of life. He was neat and
clean as never a blind man was; he never spilt
anything in eating, and was always dressed as
if he had to go to parade; you might have
thought he smelt every speck of dust on his
coat. He never cared much about eating and
drinking, but took his chief delight in delicate
perfumes; he would scent himself with essences,
and always kept plants in his room, and they

always throve with him. He would sit for hours down by the mill-stream where the weir tumbles and splashes, and the rushing noise seemed to soothe him.

The Captain was kind to the children, and it was a good thing for them to have him here too. There can be nothing better for the character of children than to be able to do little services day after day for a helpless person; it makes them well-mannered and wide awake to be obliging, and that is the best school and the best nurture for young natures.

The road-mender and the Captain died one soon after the other, without ever being really ill, either of them.

One day my father in law came home, and said to Ronymus:

"I have left my pick and hammer and rake lying up in the wood there; I don't feel exactly right, I will go and lie down. Bring me a mouthful of Kirschwasser."

He went into his room and soon after when

Ronymus went in he found his father dead. He must have died quite easily.

We took the greatest pains that the Captain should know nothing of the old man's death and burial, but he found it out and followed the body to the grave, led by Agnes. That was the last time he went out.

"Your father made the road for, other folks to walk on," he said to Ronymus as they came home; not another word, and from that time forth he spoke very little and very seldom. He had been wont to have the children with him a good deal, but now he would have no one about him but me.

"To you it was like being a daughter again, and now even that is over," he said one day. "To me—not to me—."

I well understood what he meant, but I could not tell a lie; I could not say I loved him, for I did not.

One day a letter came from Paris, and I must read it to him; the letter was from his wife, and there were dreadful things in it. The Captain was silent for a long time; then he said:

"Light a candle—burn that letter. Burn it."

I did as he desired me, and I could not but remember how my father had burnt his name.

"Give me the ashes in my hand," said the Captain. "So—it is all over. And this is what she does to me, she to whom I sacrificed every-thing. I made a great mistake. You—you—I never have done you anything but evil, and you—you have loved me. Say, do you love me? You are silent? It is right, it is honest—you have done good to me; good—." He muttered a few more words which I could not catch. I was startled and alarmed, and I called Ronymus; he came; the Captain drew a deep breath, I fell on my knees, and Ronymus closed his eyes—his dead eyes.

The Captain was buried by the side of my father-in-law the road-mender.

Well, now I have done. I don't know if any one else can say of himself that he has fulfilled the command 'Love your enemy'—I cannot say so of myself.

———

THE GOLDEN LAMB

on the sign board was already dimmed with the white vapour of a frosty dawn when Brigitta finished telling her story in the quiet hours of early morning.

Autumn was verging on winter. Thick rime lay on the graves of the Captain and the road-mender. The conduit by the house was wrapped in straw; golden ears of maize hung in the hall, and apples were stored in the now vacant rooms, perfuming the whole house. The large inn parlour was well warmed. When I took leave Brigitta accompanied me to the front steps; she hardly ever left the house, but Ronymus went with me to the station. When I told him that Brigitta had told me all her history in detail he looked at me with beaming eyes. "Am I not right," said he, "to call her the Princess of Schlehenhof?"

Just as the guard called out 'Ready' Ronymus put one more flask of Kirschwasser in
under the seat, and said:

"That is some of my oldest; some of the
first year we were here." The train rushed
past the inn of the Golden Lamb, and Brigitta
waved her hand from the steps.

.

THE END.

www.ingramcontent.com/pod-product-compliance
Lightning Source LLC
Chambersburg PA
CBHW021045030726
47496CB00006B/1699